Following His Bliss

Alex Leslie

Published by Alex Leslie, 2022.

FOLLOWING HIS BLISS

First edition. March 1, 2022.

ISBN: 979-8201988654

Written by Alex Leslie.

Table of Contents

Chapter One

THE HARSH, UNFORGIVING heat of the afternoon sun beat down on Mikey Bradshaw, as he stood next to his now worthless vehicle on the side of the desolate road. 'Road' was probably too kind of a description; an unsealed dirt track in the middle of nowhere was closer to the mark. The thick layer of compacted dry red dust that covered the track, no doubt parched from weeks without even the slightest hint of rain, cracked and baked as the sun beamed down on it relentlessly.

Having not seen a single sign of life for over an hour before the motor of his expensive new Mercedes SUV had inexplicably spluttered and died, Mikey quickly realised that, despite the dealer's assurances that this model was the ideal choice for "country life and off-road excursions," he had been sold a complete lemon, and that he could be waiting here for rescue for a very long time. The featureless dirt road extended from horizon to horizon, and in between was nothing but dirt, dust, overgrown grass and the occasional gum tree. Not a house, person or even other vehicles on the road to be seen anywhere.

Mikey could just imagine the headlines now. 'HALF-WIT CITY BOY FOUND MUMMIFIED ON COUNTRY ROAD' – or perhaps 'TREE-CHANGER FAILS TO FIND TREES, DIES ALONE IN WOOP WOOP'.

It wasn't like he hadn't prepared for this trip and it certainly wasn't an impulsive choice made at the last minute. Mikey had spent months getting ready for the big move. Easily the biggest move of his entire life. The decision to pack up his comfortable, cosmopolitan life in the bustling city of Melbourne and head for a quieter change of pace in the isolated rural town of Cooper's Landing was not taken lightly – nor had it come without serious repercussions.

From the moment he was born, Mikey was aware that his entire life had already been intricately planned out for him by his father, Randall

Bradshaw. His mother, Delia, had passed away from cancer when he was a toddler, so for most of his life, it had just been Mikey, his father, and a long parade of nannies. His father's plan for Mikey was simple. Mikey, as his only son and heir, would naturally take over his father's position as CEO of Crayborn Financial Services. There was just one slight problem – Mikey had absolutely no interest in his father's plan.

When his father had discovered from an early age that Mikey had a natural talent for numbers and mathematics, he had been elated. This was just the kind of skill a future financial trader and CEO would need. But his joy was short-lived, souring when he realised that young Mikey would much rather indulge in 'frivolous nonsense' like painting and art.

"Art is for peasants and no-hopers! Are you a no-hoper, Michael?"

From that point forward, art was considered a dirty word in the Bradshaw household. The domestic staff were under strict instructions to enforce a 'no art' rule. Mikey was forbidden to draw, paint, sculpt or even read art books. Thankfully, several of his nannies had realised what a Draconian rule this was to live under, and indulged the young boy in secret. For years, Mikey had pretended to have no interest in art, despite it being his one true love in life, all the while passionately creating and expressing himself whenever his father's back was turned. If art was a form of rebellion, then young Mikey was practically James Dean.

After his schooling was complete, Mikey was quickly thrown into an entry-level position at Crayborn Financial and the long, winding path to his destiny of becoming the company's CEO began. His natural talent for numbers meant that despite his apathy, Mikey would quickly become a remarkably talented financial trader.

His abilities meant he would go on to make his clients, and himself, wealthy beyond the dreams of avarice. When Mikey examined his most recent net holdings, after ten years of slaving away in a job he hated, he realised he had more money tucked away in bank accounts and investments than he could ever spend in three lifetimes. Thanks to some well-chosen investments earlier in his career, Mikey was the beneficiary of regular dividends that would leave him more than financially comfortable for the rest of his life – should he suddenly decide to do something crazy like quit his job and run away from his father's grand plans. But after years of being bullied into agreeing to his father's petulant demands, Mikey had all but resigned himself to his fate.

If it hadn't been for Justin.

Mikey met Justin Porter the day Mikey started at Crayborn Financial, and they had immediately bonded over work, their mutual dislike of Mikey's overbearing father, and the fact that they were both gay. There was never anything romantic between them – Justin was too much of a social butterfly for serious romantic relationships, and Mikey's eighty-hour workweeks precluded the possibility of a personal life – but they had always spent what little free time they had together, whether it be out at some new club or just hanging out at home.

Justin was everything that Mikey wished he could be. He was free-spirited. He was outspoken. He was flamboyant, egotistical and sometimes quite mean-spirited. But he also made Mikey laugh until he cried and held Mikey close when things seemed hopeless. He had been Mikey's closest friend and confidant.

As Mikey stood on the side of the deserted road, he recalled that morning six months earlier. The day he had walked into Justin's home after he had failed to show up for work, finding his best friend dead on the kitchen floor. Justin had been brutally murdered by some deranged psychopath who, thankfully, had now been caught, convicted and locked away forever.

Justin's death had left Mikey utterly devastated. It was this horrifying event that had been the catalyst for Mikey taking a good, long look at his own life and, more importantly, his priorities, and deciding that some serious changes needed to be made.

Realising for the first time that life was simply too short, Mikey was determined not to waste *his* life stuck in a soul-crushing job that he hated with a passion. He wasn't ungrateful for the opportunities his father had provided him with, but Mikey resented the lack of control in his life; the fact that he couldn't choose his own path or have a say in his own destiny. His earliest memories were of his father lecturing him on the importance of the company and how the company must always come first. Mikey might have subscribed to this philosophy if he had voluntarily chosen to become part of the company, but since his entire life had been dedicated to one day becoming CEO without anyone bothering to ask if that was something Mikey wanted, it was difficult for him to feel any obligation to the company, let alone elevating it above Mikey's own happiness and well-being.

Mikey wanted freedom. He wanted to make his own choices. He wanted to escape from his father's plans. But more than anything – Mikey wanted to paint. His passion for art had never died, despite his father's best efforts to kill it during his childhood. When Mikey moved out of home at the age of nineteen, his need to hide his artistic pursuits became less important. It wasn't like his father dropped around to socialise regularly. But his stifling work hours meant that he rarely had time to express himself. He'd tried getting his father to agree to a more reasonable work schedule, but this subject had been shut down anytime Mikey had felt brave enough to raise it.

"You don't become a success by slacking off!"

After Justin died, Mikey took a few weeks off from work. It had been the first leave he had taken in his entire career. His father had strongly protested, but it was clear that Mikey's grief had meant he was not in a fit state of mind to be playing around with other people's money. God knew his father didn't want to endanger his precious company's reputation by having his grieving son make a mistake and bankrupt a wealthy client, so he begrudgingly allowed the leave request to go through.

It was during this time off that Mikey began formulating his plans. He wanted to leave Crayborn Financial. He wanted to escape the straight lines and grey concrete of the city. He wanted to be surrounded by nature. He loathed the cliché expressions of 'tree-change' or 'following his bliss,' but such a lifestyle shift was exactly what he needed. He wanted to be free to pursue his art, enjoy a slower pace of life and take the time to enjoy himself for the first time. He sat in his bed, laptop open, and crunched the numbers. He could easily do it. He just needed to settle on the specifics.

Mikey knew he would have to leave Melbourne altogether. Simply moving to the suburbs wasn't going to be enough to escape his father's influence. God knew the moment he resigned from the company, his dear old Dad would explode, and a campaign to get his son back to work would soon begin. But, if distance meant his father would have to take time off work in order to pursue such a campaign rather than him simply sending his staff across the city to do his bidding, it may die before it even begins.

After researching several real estate websites, Mikey eventually found a gorgeous old ranch house on the outskirts of a tiny little town called Cooper's Landing. At around eight hours drive from the heart of Melbourne, the town was far enough away from his father that Mikey wouldn't have to worry about him dropping by daily to harass him, and the location was perfect for Mikey's needs. Rural, isolated and beautiful judging by the photographs he had seen online, Cooper's Landing was as far from a concrete jungle as you could get, and the house prices were ridiculously cheap compared to the city. Mikey contacted the agent and arranged to do a virtual tour. Within days, he was digitally signing the contracts and his new life was set to begin. There was just one last thing to do – hand in his notice to his father.

"Is this some kind of joke, Michael?" his father had said, slamming Mikey's written resignation down on his desk. The sound resonated off the office walls.

"Not at all, Father. I'm done. This isn't what I want for my life. I want to explore my own path."

"But painting? Where's the money in that? The art world is just a bunch of swindlers and poseurs. How can you expect to be a success?"

"It's not about being a success. It's about doing what feels right. It's about waking up in the morning and not wishing the day was already over. It's about being happy."

"Happy doesn't pay the bills!"

"No, but it makes life worth living..."

The rest of the meeting descended into little more than his father tearing him to shreds, calling him ungrateful, and swearing up and down that Mikey would eventually come crawling back, penniless and on his hands and knees, begging for forgiveness. Mikey let his father's venom wash over him, knowing in that moment that he had made the right decision. If Randall Bradshaw was more interested in his son being rich than happy, then Mikey knew there was no further point in trying to make the man understand. He simply walked out of his father's office when the old man had finished blustering, packed up his desk and left Crayborn Financial for the last time.

The heat of the sun broke Mikey away from his internal reverie, and he realised he would have to do something soon or he was going to end up with sunstroke. He tried his phone, but just like the GPS in the vehicle, he was outside of the service network. His phone carrier frequently advertised how its network covers 98% of Australia – so trust Mikey to break down smack dab in the middle of the 2%.

He popped the hood and surveyed the engine bay. He checked the oil, fiddled with wires, and after ten minutes of studying the motor, decided he knew less about cars than he had ten minutes earlier. He closed the bonnet and grabbed some water from the back of his over-stuffed SUV.

Since Mikey's Melbourne apartment had come fully furnished, he hadn't needed to go to the trouble of hiring a moving truck. His clothes, electronics and personal items all fitted, albeit tightly, in the newly purchased SUV. His new home was unfurnished, but he was happy to rough it in a sleeping bag for a few days while he sourced some new furniture locally and ordered any other household items online.

Not that he would ever need new furniture if he didn't figure out how to get the damned car started. But a noise in the distance heralded salvation. A car, travelling in the same direction as Mikey, appeared on the distant horizon in a cloud of red dust. Mikey turned on the SUV's hazard lights and started blasting the horn to get the driver's attention.

As the other vehicle approached, Mikey recognised the distinctive white and blue four-wheel drive as it came into focus. A police vehicle. Mikey's last interaction with the police had been shortly after he found Justin. The unhappy memory came swiftly to the surface, but Mikey did his best to push it back down. He focused on getting the cop's attention. Hopefully, they could at least radio for a tow truck or give him a lift to somewhere with a telephone. Although he was sure he wasn't that far from Cooper's Landing. Mikey had deliberately left Melbourne before dawn, not wanting to get stuck on unfamiliar country roads at night. When the GPS had died earlier that day, he had been no more than two hours drive away from his destination.

His persistent honking paid off, and the cop flashed his lights in acknowledgement, slowing as he approached and pulling over directly behind Mikey's stranded vehicle. A tall, well-built man with short, dark hair got out of the vehicle, put on his police hat and sunglasses and approached Mikey slowly. His dark navy blue pants moulded perfectly to his thick, trunk-like thighs. His short-sleeved, light blue uniform shirt was similarly well fitted, however seemed to be straining slightly at the upper arms. The cop wasn't a muscle-bound god, but he was certainly toned; covered with thick, ropey muscles that were coiled and ready to spring into action. A body that had been toned through hard work and an active lifestyle – not protein shakes and a six-day-a-week gym addiction.

Mikey shook his head slightly and came to his senses. Stopping his visual assessment of the man, he awkwardly looked away. He wasn't in the middle of some city nightclub, on the hunt for a hookup. Openly ogling some random country cop on a deserted road in the middle of nowhere was not the smartest choice Mikey could make – especially if he wanted to get out of here in one piece.

The man gave off a hard-as-nails, alpha male kind of vibe, which was both sexy and intimidating. However, Mikey suspected this vibe was as much a part of his uniform as his hat or holster belt. He also couldn't help noticing the cop had been watching him closely like a hawk too. Although Mikey had to assume that was the action of a cop assessing a potentially dangerous situation.

"G'day," the cop said with the kind of gruff, masculine voice that came only from being born and bred in the country, "Having car trouble are ya, mate?"

"Yeah," Mikey replied, "She just died on me and I've been stuck here for about two hours. I couldn't get any phone service to call for help."

"You're just outside mobile range. Walk fifteen minutes that way and you'll get full reception," the cop said, pointing toward the road ahead. "Where are you headed?"

"Cooper's Landing. Do you know it?"

The cop chuckled and extended his hand, "Sergeant Wayne Townsend. Cooper's Landing Police." Mikey took the man's hand and shook it firmly and assertively.

"Michael Bradshaw. But my friends call me Mikey."

"Well, Mikey, Cooper's Landing is only about ninety minutes away. You visiting family?"

"Um, actually, I live there. Or I will if I ever get there. Today's moving day." Mikey gestured to the SUV stuffed to the gills with his personal possessions.

"Really?" Wayne said, sounding surprised, "Well, it'll be nice to see a new face in town. We don't get many newcomers."

When Wayne smiled, his whole stance seemed to relax. Mikey felt an instant hit of warmth in his chest. The country cop was friendly despite his initial gruffness. His tough guy, alpha male facade had apparently fallen away now that he had determined that Mikey wasn't a threat.

"Pop the hood," Wayne ordered, "Let's see if we can't get this heap of junk going again."

"Hey! She's brand new AND top of the line!" Mikey protested indignantly.

"Top of the line for dropping your kids off at some fancy inner-city private school, maybe. But off-roading? Gimme a break! These European deathtraps fall apart the moment you take them off a sealed road..." he said as he fiddled with some component deep in the engine bay.

"The dealer told me it was perfect for country life!" Mikey tried to defend his expensive lemon.

"The dealer saw you coming..." Wayne grunted as he pulled the uncooperative part free, "There! That's your problem. Your air filter is loaded with crud. Dirt from the unsealed road gets tossed up into the engine bay as you drive over it. This thing was never designed to handle that kind of punishment."

Mikey was impressed. He had no idea what the man had just said, but it sounded convincing. That being said, with Mikey's lack of mechanical knowledge, Wayne could have told him the car broke down due to a lack of rainbows and pixy dust, and he wouldn't have been any the wiser.

"Can it be fixed?"

"In the short term. Rinse this out with some water and let it dry. It should get you as far as Cooper's. But in the long term, you're gonna wanna think about getting yourself a more suitable vehicle, like a ute or a proper four-wheel drive. If you're gonna be staying out here long term, that is."

Mikey grabbed the bottle of water and did his best to rinse the dirt out of the filter. He made short work of it, and within a few minutes, the harsh heat of the sun had the part dry and ready to be reseated in the engine bay. Wayne pulled a cotton handkerchief out of his pocket and wiped his greasy hands clean.

"Turn her over. Let's see if we've done it." Wayne ordered. Mikey opened the driver's door, tried not to pass out from the wall of heat that had built up in the car, and turned the key. The engine spluttered to life. Mikey cheered with excitement, and Wayne closed the hood with a resounding thud.

"Thank you so much, Sergeant. You're a lifesaver!" Mikey said, unable to wipe the smile from his face.

"You're very welcome. Now get moving. I have no idea if that filter will last long, but at least if you break down again, you'll have phone reception," Wayne handed him a business card, "If you do break down, this is my number. Call me and I'll bring the cavalry."

"Fingers crossed I'll make it back to the sealed road soon. Thanks again." Mikey said as he turned toward his vehicle.

"Oh, one last thing?"

Mikey turned back and noticed that Wayne immediately stiffened as if startled by something. It lasted only a second, after which Wayne seemed to loosen back up, but his voice had returned to its former, more official tone.

"Welcome to Cooper's Landing," Wayne said gruffly, then without another word, he returned to his vehicle, as if he were suddenly in a hurry.

Mikey smiled as the country cop quickly pulled away, leaving a cloud of red dust in his wake, and once again Mikey was alone on the side of the road. With the engine running smoothly for the moment, Mikey decided not to chance it by sticking around any longer. He pulled back onto the road and resumed his journey to Cooper's Landing.

~

It was almost two hours later when Mikey finally made it to his destination. Once the GPS came back online, he was directed to drive through Cooper's Landing, then turn off the main highway onto yet another dirt track. The expansive, single floor ranch house came into view at the end of a tree-lined, dirt track driveway.

The house had been built in the early 1900s but had stood abandoned and unoccupied since the early seventies. Originally one of over a dozen similar ranches that lined the northern end of Cooper's Landing, Mikey's new home was the last one standing; the others having long since been demolished. The previous owners had bought the property for a song and done a quick renovation to make it habitable.

Even having been recently renovated, the house had been a bargain. A house this size in the city would have cost at least ten times what Mikey had paid for it. Pulling the SUV up near the front door, since there was no paved driveway or specific parking area, Mikey jumped out and admired his new home.

The exterior had been repainted in warm cream tones with dark green accents. The wide porch extended all the way around the house, as was typical of houses of this vintage. The corrugated iron roof was freshly restored with dark, rust-tinted paint. Overall, the four-bedroom home was enormous for just one person. But having lived in the city, where space was always at a premium, the idea of rattling around in a huge old house was a luxury Mikey was looking forward to enjoying.

After opening the front door and stepping inside, it was clear the house had lain empty for a while. Inside was stale and in desperate need of airing. Mikey wandered around, opening all the doors and windows, allowing the cool afternoon breeze to clear away the stuffiness. He then quickly unloaded everything from the SUV.

Since the house was unfurnished and totally empty, he wasn't concerned about anything for the moment other than getting everything inside. He dumped the suitcases containing his clothes in one of the bedrooms. He dug out the bag containing his toiletries and personal grooming items and put them in the bathroom. Everything else was dumped unceremoniously on the living room floor.

By the time Mikey was finished, the sun had set and the temperature had dropped significantly. He set about closing all the open windows and doors, the house now smelling a lot fresher than it had, and headed to the kitchen.

Along with the bathrooms, the kitchen had been completely renovated and modernised. Currently, all that was installed were the main fixtures. The oven, stovetop and fridge were all in place, as was the huge, country style sink. But beyond that, all the kitchen could offer a weary traveller like Mikey was running water and empty cupboards.

It was then Mikey realised he had failed to pack any food or cooking supplies. In the city, Mikey didn't have time to cook. He mostly lived off takeaway or food deliveries. He guessed that neither of them was going to be an option there. He could have driven into town and picked up something to eat, but he was so exhausted after such a long day of driving, the idea was not in the least bit appealing.

Mikey decided an early night was probably the best choice. He unpacked a change of clothes and took a long, hot shower in the main bathroom. The high-pressure showerhead kneaded his tired muscles into submission and left him feeling relaxed and ready for a good night's sleep. Although, he wasn't sure how good of a sleep he was likely to get in a roll-out sleeping bag on the floor. But after the day he'd had, he would have slept soundly on a bed of nails at that point.

Once dried, changed and ready for bed, Mikey set up the sleeping bag and a couple of his favourite pillows on the living room floor. He plugged his phone in to charge and wriggled his way into his makeshift bed. The silence was strange. No traffic. No people making noises everywhere. Just an eerie kind of natural stillness. Mikey couldn't deal with that much quiet. He set his phone to play some soft classical music, lay back and closed his eyes. As the music filled the air, Mikey relaxed and was fast asleep within minutes.

Chapter Two

AFTER HELPING THE handsome city boy get his overpriced piece of junk started, Sergeant Wayne Townsend resumed his highway patrol duties, pulling away carefully and watching in the rear vision mirror as Mikey slowly disappeared from view.

Wayne had been entranced by Mikey from the moment he laid eyes on him. That soft, dark blond hair; that smooth, pale skin; those blue eyes, bluer than a summer sky and brighter than sunshine. A few years younger than Wayne, the newcomer had a lightly toned physique; lean, like a swimmer or a diver. Wayne had tried not to be too obvious in his observations, eternally thanking his ever-present sunglasses which blocked the view of his wandering eyes.

Wayne chastised himself for being such a chickenshit. He had fully intended to ask the handsome stranger out, but had quickly changed his mind at the last second. Partly because he couldn't be sure if Mikey was, in fact, gay; and partly because Wayne was concerned that hitting on a guy he had just rescued from being stuck in the middle of nowhere might be seen by some as a bit of a creeper move.

The latter reason was legitimate, but Wayne wasn't so sure about the former, feeling like it was just a flimsy excuse to cover his cowardice. After all, Wayne's gaydar was pretty well-tuned, and Mikey had definitely given off more than a couple of blips. But just as Wayne was summoning the courage to ask him out for a drink, it suddenly occurred to him that his gaydar had only ever been used on 'country' gays; men who didn't necessarily give off any obvious outward signs of their homosexuality, but would give away their orientation subtly when they laughed at certain jokes or showed certain facial expressions. Wayne couldn't be sure the usual 'tells' would work on gays from the big city.

From Wayne's limited experience with city men, the usual cues that would set off his gaydar could easily be misconstrued. He was generalising, of course, but city men were usually less rough-and-tumble and more metrosexual than the average country guy. The cute stranger, while far from being effeminate or stereotypically 'queer' in nature, did give off certain vibes. But was he actually gay? Or was Wayne simply misconstruing a soft, city boy's lack of country life experience? Until he was sure, Wayne felt, at that moment, that it was probably best not to declare his intentions.

At least, that's the excuse he was going with.

The younger man had clearly made the worst possible choice when it came to vehicles, especially in these harsh, rural conditions. Wayne hoped Mikey would heed his advice and look at getting something more reliable in the near future. He didn't like the idea of Cooper's Landing's newest resident being in need of emergency rescue before the poor guy had even unpacked.

Wayne sighed to himself. He couldn't help but feel that his interaction with the city boy, brief though it was, would no doubt be the highlight of the day. As Cooper's Landing's only police officer, Wayne was responsible for protecting and serving what was possibly Australia's sleepiest country town. With a population of just over 500 permanent residents, Cooper's Landing was far from being a sordid hotbed of criminal activity and intrigue. Wayne's duties mostly consisted of highway patrol, resolving minor neighbourhood disputes and breaking up the occasional fight at the pub when a few of the patrons had one too many beers.

With it getting late in the day and having completed another full circuit of the town, Wayne returned to the police station to check-in. Situated just off Main Street, the old station house was a classic sandstone building constructed in the early 1900s. The front section featured the main offices and reception area. The remainder of the structure, including the cells and watch house in the rear, were no longer in use.

Since the funding cutbacks a few years ago left Wayne as the only permanent officer assigned to the station, the cells couldn't be officially used as there would be no one to supervise any prisoners whenever Wayne had to leave the building. The watch house, a small apartment designed for an officer to live in full-time while they performed the overnight prisoner supervisory duties, was technically free for Wayne to use. But when he first started working at Cooper's Landing Police, he had quickly elected to find his own house to live in. It didn't take him long to discover the watch house was simply too small to live in long term. Besides, it was hard to get any kind of privacy if your workplace also happened to be your home.

Parking his vehicle in his assigned space out the front of the station, Wayne strode in the front door and passed the reception desk. Old Shirl, the station's office assistant and radio operator, was sitting at the reception desk, talking on the phone.

Shirl had been working at the Cooper's Landing Police Station for as long as anyone could remember. In her late sixties, she was the quintessential rural woman. Hard as nails but with a heart of gold, Shirl was tough but possessed a generosity of spirit that only came from a lifetime in a country town. Despite numerous attempts to get rid of her by the bean counters in Melbourne, Wayne had fought hard to keep Shirl on as his office assistant. He'd had to make more than a few budgetary sacrifices over the years in order to keep her on, but her dedication to the job and local knowledge meant she was worth every penny.

On a personal level, Shirl was very much an individual. A lifelong bachelorette, she had the voice and appearance of a cockatoo, and the dress sense of a 1970's drag queen. Her hair was thin, like finely spun toffee, and was teased into a permanent beehive. Her makeup consisted of dark blue eye shadow and coral pink lipstick. The look was completed by one of her trademark faux silk kaftans. Today's was a flowing bright green number with red splashes, giving the appearance that she was on her way to perform a Christmas show with Les Girls.

Wayne suspected that Shirl was simply one of those people who found a look that worked for her at an early age, then simply stuck with it, regardless of how fashion tastes had changed. His grandfather has been much the same, having adopted the 'teddy boy' look of the 1950s and maintained it until the day he died. Wayne wasn't one to judge. If Shirl was happy, that's all that mattered. Although, he could do without those days when the wind would blow her kaftan up unexpectedly, revealing whether or not his office assistant had remembered to put on underwear that morning.

"Oh sure, love," Shirl said to the caller, "I'll send him on over when he's finished up here. You keep out of trouble and I'll catch up with you later!" she said with a throaty laugh as she hung up the phone.

"Let me guess," Wayne said, as he headed to the kitchenette and began making both himself and Shirl some coffee, "The anti-terrorist squad has finally classified Mrs Patterson's beef casserole as a biological weapon, and they want me to take her into custody?"

Shirl chuckled, "Not today, pet. Your mother wants you to drop around after work."

Wayne grimaced.

"Now, be nice! I'm sure she just wants to catch up."

"Yeah, I'm sure..." Wayne muttered, "I can just imagine it now," he said, affecting what he believed to be a dead-on impression of Mavis Townsend, "Oh, darling! I met the most delightful man for you at the community centre! He's ninety-seven years old and I don't think he's gay... but you never know!"

"She's not that bad!" Shirl squawked with laughter.

"Perhaps not, but she has been relentless recently. It seems every time I speak with her, the subject of my love life comes up. I swear if I go around there tonight and it's another of her famous fix-ups..."

"She's just worried about you," Shirl said understandingly, "Mavis loves you and wants you to be happy. She doesn't like the idea of you spending your life alone."

"She doesn't understand. It's not so easy for guys like me. She sees her friend's sons getting married and having kids, and she wants that for me. But she can never fully grasp that it's harder for gay guys in rural areas. Our options are a lot more limited. Besides, not everyone wants to deal with the drama of spending their life with a cop."

Shirl snorted derisively at him, "Poppycock! The old sergeant was married for forty years."

"To a woman."

"That's beside the point. He found someone, and you will too. Alright, it might take you a little longer. But one day, the man of your dreams will show up and sweep you off your feet!" Shirl said dramatically.

Wayne found himself smiling to himself. He quickly schooled his features, but the shrewd older woman didn't miss a beat.

"I saw that! Perhaps Mr Right has already shown up. Am I right?"

"Oh, look at the time! I really must be heading off. I don't want to keep Mum waiting!" Wayne said with a cheeky smile, handing Shirl her coffee and making a hasty retreat toward the front door.

"Alright, but you can't avoid me forever. I want details!"

Wayne chuckled nervously as he made his escape outside, jumping into his 4WD and departing as quickly as he could.

~

More than anything, Wayne just wanted to go home. He could have a nice, long, hot shower; get into some comfortable, casual clothes; switch on the TV and crash out on the couch. However, ignoring a summons from Mavis Townsend would not be advisable. So he bit the bullet and headed towards her home; the house Wayne grew up in.

Wayne loved his mother very much. Despite her constant interference in his personal life and her gossipy nature, she was his whole world. The only living family he had left since his father passed away when he was fifteen, Mavis was everything he could ever ask for in a mother. That being said, Wayne had learned that a little bit of Mavis went a long way, especially once she had taken it upon herself to find her only son a boyfriend.

It was embarrassing more than anything; having his mother getting her fellow gossips in town to report in with any dating possibilities. Particularly when no one in her little gossip network could spot a gay man to save their lives. Thankfully, the vast majority of straight men in Cooper's Landing were more than understanding when one of the gossip gestapo would mistakenly try to set them up on a date with the local police sergeant. Most of them had been set up on more than a few disastrous dates over the years by the same group of clueless women. With their appalling strike rate, it was a wonder that the population of Cooper's Landing wasn't in terminal decline.

As soon as Wayne opened the front door and stepped inside, Wayne was immediately engulfed in a strong embrace by his mother. Standing at just five feet (with heels on) and with a slim, willowy figure, Mavis Townsend did not immediately command a formidable presence. But what she lacked in size, she made up for in personality.

If Old Shirl had based her appearance on a seventies disco queen, Wayne's mother had based hers on a stereotypical fifties TV housewife. Despite the style being decades old by the time she adopted it, Mavis had always worn the type of conservative style of a Donna Reid or Mrs Cleaver. Tidy, pulled back hair; crisp, well-ironed dresses and she was never without a brilliantly white lace-trimmed apron whenever cooking in the kitchen.

"Oh, darling! I'm so glad you're here. How was work today? No, don't answer yet. Come and sit down at the table, dinner is ready."

With that, Mavis Townsend released him from her vice-like grip and darted away to the kitchen. Wayne inhaled and was hit with the aroma of roasting meat. Following in his mother's wake, Wayne entered the kitchen and sat down at the dining table. Laid out in front of him was roast beef with all the trimmings. Mavis had even gone to the trouble to make real Yorkshire puddings and a gloriously thick jug of gravy. All his favourites.

She was up to something. Wayne could feel it.

Mavis handed him a plate, heavily laden with large portions of everything. Easily enough food to choke a horse. Wayne wasn't about to complain. He loved a good Sunday roast, even if it wasn't Sunday. He took a bite of the succulent, perfectly cooked meat and it melted in his mouth. No one made a roast like his Mum.

As they both ate, Mavis brought Wayne up-to-date on all the latest gossip from around Cooper's Landing. He did his best not to roll his eyes, since he couldn't care less who the Mayor was secretly shagging, or who was suspected of submitting a store-bought cake to the CWA's cake decorating competition. Wayne waited until he was about halfway done with his meal before finally confronting the elephant in the room.

"So, what are you up to, Mum? The only time you mysteriously summon me at the last minute AND make me all my favourite foods is when you're up to something. So, what do you want?"

His mother made a very good attempt at looking scandalised at her son's outrageously suspicious nature. With her dramatic abilities, Wayne firmly believed that in another time and place, Mavis Townsend would have given Meryl Streep a run for her money.

"I don't know what you mean, darling!" Mavis said breathlessly.

"Come on, Mum, 'fess up!" Wayne groaned.

"Oh, alright. I think I may have found your Mr Right!"

Wayne couldn't stop himself from rolling his eyes. Mavis immediately slapped him on the arm, "Don't disrespect your mother!" she said sharply.

"Ow!" Wayne cried dramatically as if mortally wounded by his mother's withering attack, "Cut that out, or I'll charge you with child abuse!"

"Rubbish!" his mother dismissed with a smirk, "Real child abuse would be not letting you have any of my special pav for dessert..."

With that, Wayne was stopped in his tracks. His Mum's pavlova was the stuff of legend and being denied such a rare treat would be a cruel and unusual punishment. So he did what any smart son would do: he shut his trap and listened to his mother.

"I met him down at the community centre. He's a little older than your usual type, but age is just a number..."

Wayne cut her off, "Mum, stop. When are you going to learn to stop doing this? Let me handle my own personal life for once!"

"What personal life?" Mavis said, slightly venomously. Wayne scowled at her. It was bad enough knowing he didn't have a personal life, he didn't need his mother reminding him. Mavis, at least, looked contrite the moment the savage words left her lips.

"Darling, I'm sorry. That was uncalled for. I didn't mean to say that. Please forgive me."

Wayne nodded stiffly, still a little wounded by his mother's unprovoked use of that particular truth bomb.

"You never talk about your personal life, so I never know if you're seeing anyone or not. *Is* there someone special?"

Wayne smiled to himself as the memory of the cute city boy from earlier that day suddenly came to mind.

"What's his name?"

"Mikey. But he isn't anyone special. I don't even know him. He just moved to town today. I ran into him out on the highway after his car broke down. I don't even know if he's gay. But... he was nice."

Mavis smiled wide, as if pleased her son had finally found someone. A little premature given that Wayne had barely had one conversation with the man.

"You leave it to me, darling. I'll find out everything about him and report back ASAP!"

"Mum, no! Don't get involved. I don't want you trying to fix me up with him. The poor guy has just moved to town. We don't want to scare him away if he isn't gay and the entire town suddenly starts trying to set him up with me."

"Relax. I promise, strictly recon only. *Recon!* I sound like something out of those silly army movies you used to watch as a kid." his Mum giggled as she cleared the plates from the dining table.

Wayne attempted to intervene further but was quickly cut off mid-sentence when Mavis returned to the table baring a glorious Pavlova topped with mounds of soft whipped cream and fresh fruit. He quickly lost any capacity for logical thought as his mother cut him a suitably large slice of the decadent meringue dessert.

After eating, Wayne was sent home armed with several plastic containers stuffed with leftovers and some more pavlova. He knew that his mother's involvement in his love life was usually guaranteed to end in disaster, but since she had promised that, on this occasion, she would be extra discreet in her information gathering, Wayne could only hope that Mavis and her gossip collective could operate with at least some degree of subtlety.

Chapter Three

MIKEY WOKE UP on the living room floor in a crumpled heap. The bright morning light streamed through the edges of the curtains and lace netting that barely covered the huge front-facing window.

He fumbled for his phone, finding it on the floor next to him, and was shocked to see it was well after 9 AM. Mikey couldn't remember the last time he had slept so long, or so late. Normally, he'd be up before dawn getting through his morning routine, then off to the office to catch up on the overnight financial markets. The idea of being able to sleep in like this was so alien but strangely seductive.

Mikey felt he could really get used to it.

He carefully extracted himself from the sleeping bag and soon discovered, when his back started twinging that, despite the hefty price tag at the city camping store, the sleeping bag he had bought had not provided anywhere near enough padding. After a few minutes of gentle stretching, Mikey's lower back felt slightly less like a poorly maintained wire coat hanger and he was able to stand up. A new bed with a proper mattress had just rocketed to the top of today's 'must-buy' list, so Mikey needed to get himself ready and hit the town.

After collecting his toiletries bag and a change of clothes from the bedroom, Mikey stepped into the steaming hot shower and felt the remaining knots in his back melt away. The mint and tea tree body wash left a cool tingle on his skin that was both refreshing and invigorating. Mikey took his time, enjoying the heat of the shower. Although he had a lot to do that day, he had no reason to rush around like his life in the city. For the first time, he could take things as they came. A wide smile came unexpectedly to his face. His choice to move here was already making him happier.

Once dried and dressed, Mikey headed out to the kitchen for some breakfast. However, he had forgotten that he had not yet had a chance to go into town to get supplies. There was no food or coffee in his bare kitchen cupboards, and the fridge held only empty ice cube trays. Mikey frowned. Before he could do anything, he would need coffee. Showers were great, but his brain did not function well without caffeine.

Mikey grabbed his wallet, keys and phone then headed out to the SUV, a plan forming in his head. First, find somewhere for breakfast, then a day of shopping for his new home. Whatever he couldn't find in town, he would order online when he got home. Being able to buy just about anything on the internet and have it show up on your doorstep only a few days later was one of those modern marvels Mikey was eternally grateful for.

~

In the weeks leading up to the big move, Mikey had studied satellite maps of Cooper's Landing online so he would at least have a rough idea of where everything was before he got there. The town wasn't a big place. If Main Street was the centre, then Mikey's place was at the northernmost boundary, about a 10-minute drive from the town itself. To the south, the Gurangajin river ran the length of the town. To the east was the main highway out of town leading to the neighbouring town of Bushman's Pass. Finally, in the west of town, the river bent around the base of some small, green hills, then snaked its way inland.

There was virtually nothing between the ranch and Main Street. Mostly just untamed scrubland and hundreds of gum trees. The drive was quiet, with no other vehicles in sight until he approached the western end of town. He saw two battered old utes stopped at an intersection. Both the drivers were insisting that the other had right of way. Mikey chuckled to himself, enjoying the thought that this was apparently 'rush hour' in Cooper's Landing. Once the other drivers had moved on, Mikey continued and noticed as he headed onto Main Street how many people were driving utes and similar working trucks. He was reminded of the advice from Sergeant Townsend the day before. Mikey would need to look into replacing his car soon. But first things first: coffee.

Mikey pulled over and parked in one of the angle parking spaces outside a modern looking cafe. The building looked a lot newer than the majority of shops on Main Street. The sign above the entryway had caught Mikey's attention, and his curiosity forced him to check it out.

'Grinder Boys' was a cool little cafe that wouldn't look out of place in the Melbourne CBD, but seemed completely incongruous amongst the early 20th Century buildings that surrounded it. Mikey was relieved that anything even remotely resembling a cafe existed in Cooper's Landing. Mikey would not cope well without coffee, and making it from scratch at home was a pain in the arse. The name of the business made Mikey smile, and he wondered if the owner had any idea how queer their cafe sounded. He stepped inside and quickly realised the name was not an accident.

The cafe was virtually deserted, the main morning rush apparently having happened hours ago. The interior was dominated by black and chrome. The tables, chairs and menus looked almost like they had been lifted straight out of a BDSM club. It only took one look at the two men who ran the place to realise why. Both mid-forties; both with full sleeve tattoos on their arms, proudly shown off, courtesy of their matching black muscle shirts; both men looked more like they should be in a motorcycle gang rather than slinging cappuccinos. The only major point of difference in their outfits were the bandanas they wore around their necks. The man standing behind the counter, wiping down the coffee machine, wore blue. The other, slightly gruffer-looking man, who was headed out the back to what Mikey presumed was the kitchen, wore red.

"You must be Mikey!" Blue exclaimed loudly, shaking Mikey from his reverie.

"Um, yeah, I am. How did you know?"

"You're the new guy in town." Blue said with a wide smile, as if that explained everything, "We don't get a lot of new people in town, so when it happens, it's kind of a big deal. The whole town is talking about you. I'm Sean, by the way," he said, holding his hand out to shake.

Mikey shook his hand, feeling the firm grip of the other man's surprisingly smooth skin. Mikey wasn't sure how to feel about having the entire town talking about him, but he figured it was only to be expected. With a population of around 500 people, a new arrival was likely to draw some attention. But being scrutinised by everyone only one day after arriving? He would have to make sure he didn't do anything weird or embarrassing, otherwise his reputation in town could be destroyed before he had even had the chance to unpack.

"Well, can I have a triple shot latte on skim, please?"

Sean looked at him like he had grown a second head, "Um, are you sure about that?"

"Sure about what?"

"It's just, well, no one has ever ordered a triple shot anything before. That's a *lot* of caffeine, you know?"

"Well, you better get used to me ordering it,' Mikey said with a grin, "I *live* on caffeine and anything less than a triple shot, well I might as well order a glass of water."

Sean seemed visibly uncomfortable about complying with Mikey's request, almost as if he was itching to argue his point about the excessive caffeine, but he nodded tightly and complied.

"Did you want breakfast, too?"

"I'll have a toasted ham and cheese croissant, please."

Sean shouted out the order to the other man, who responded with a loud, baritone voice "On it!" while Sean started work on the coffee machine. Within moments, Sean was handing Mikey his latte. Mikey took a sip and groaned his appreciation.

"So," Sean asked as he wiped down the counter, "What's a nice city boy like you doing in a country town like this?"

"Well, I'm hoping to make a few positive changes. Life's been a bit hectic lately, and I could really use a slower pace. Where better to do that than a gorgeous little town amongst this picturesque landscape?"

"I hope you don't mind me asking," Sean said, looking a little uncomfortable, "but are you, by any chance, gay?"

Mikey was immediately on alert. Had he been reading too much into the signage and the cafe's décor? Were these guys who looked like they should be in a motorcycle gang *actually* in a motorcycle gang? Was he about to get into a violent confrontation? Mikey's brain short-circuited and, of course, said what was possibly the stupidest thing he could in such a situation.

"Why, are you offering?"

Mikey immediately started berating himself in his head for being such a fucking idiot.

Sean looked at him, clearly not expecting that response. But the slow grin that spread across his face did not suggest he was offended in the slightest. However, when the other man with the red bandana came storming out of the backroom, carrying what Mikey presumed was his toasted croissant, the look he got was nothing short of withering.

"Are you hitting on my man?" Red boomed, scowling.

Mikey attempted to sputter a response, but as Red came closer, Mikey began to panic. How exactly did he get himself into these situations? Was he seriously about to get beaten up by a gay motorcycle gang before breakfast?

Red slammed the plate down on the vacant table Mikey was standing next to. Mikey flinched and Red smiled wickedly.

"We only play together, boy!" Red said gruffly, looking Mikey up and down. Sean came over and slapped Red on the arm.

"Stop teasing him, Scott! Mikey, please forgive him. We've been out of the lifestyle for a few years now, but my partner here still has trouble reigning in his big bad Dom persona."

Scott turned to face Sean, his look incredulous, "*My* big bad Dom persona? What about yours! You threatened to spank the milkman last week!"

"He forgot the soy milk again,' Sean said evenly, "I warned him there would be consequences..."

Mikey cleared his throat. The two men stopped arguing and looked at him.

"This is the best cafe EVER!" Mikey squealed. Sean and Scott both blushed, beaming at their customer's praise. Mikey sat down at the table and enjoyed his coffee and croissant. He was happy that not only were there other gay people in town, but they also were not planning on beating him to a bloody pulp before breakfast. Well, not unless he really wanted them to.

~

After breakfast, Mikey asked the Grinder Boys if there was a furniture store in town. They directed him to a store called 'Harrison's' located at the other end of Main Street. He jumped in his SUV and made his way leisurely down the middle of town. With little traffic, the trip took less than two minutes. He pulled up outside a large storefront with an ornate, hand-carved wooden sign suspended above the door by brass chains. In the front windows, beautiful antique wooden furniture was displayed alongside matching modern pieces. Mikey was positive he would be able to get at least some of the furniture items he needed for the house plus, hopefully, a bed.

Stepping inside, the store was filled with an extraordinary range of furniture, both old, new and restored, along with accessories and various decorative pieces. Mikey headed toward the back of the store where various beds were on display.

"You must be Mikey," a warm, purring voice announced from behind a china cabinet. Mikey flinched, but relaxed when a statuesque redhead in her sixties emerged, her smile as warm as her voice. She was wearing a well-worn pair of jeans and a polo top with the store's name printed across the chest.

"I'm sorry," she said, "I didn't mean to sneak up on you. I'm Sandra Harrison. Welcome to my store."

"Thank you. Mikey Bradshaw. It's a pleasure to meet you," he said, regaining his composure. Sandra smiled wide and shook his hand.

"Were you looking for anything in particular, or just browsing?"

"Well, I need some furniture for my new house. The priority is bedroom and living room stuff for the moment. I'll get to the rest later."

"I'm sure I can help you find what you need. What's your address?"

Mikey gave her the address and she quickly wrote it down on a small notebook she pulled out of her back pocket.

"Oh, that's the old Riverside Ranch. I had no idea anyone had bought it."

"*Riverside* Ranch?" Mikey said, confused, "But... isn't the river on the other side of town?"

"It is now," Sandra chuckled lightly, "Back in the 1970s, the council diverted the river to the south side of town. That's where most of the farms and ranches were at the time and still are today. Since there was only a small number of farms on the north side, it made more sense to divert the river, than have dozens of farms on the south side operating off the town's water supply."

"Wow. I had no idea. All I knew was the ranch had been abandoned long ago. I like the name, but I suppose it doesn't make much sense to use it these days."

"Probably not," Sandra laughed, "But since I'm familiar with the property, I think I can point out some lovely pieces that should go well with your home. Let's start with the bedroom."

Over the next hour, Mikey and Sandra wandered around the store looking at some exceptional pieces. Most of Sandra's wares were strangely inexpensive. While Mikey wasn't an expert in antiques, he would be surprised if this stuff wouldn't sell for a lot more down in

Melbourne. Mikey simply assumed that while much of her stock was 'old' it was probably not 'antique' – or possibly it was all a bunch of cheap knock-offs. Regardless, Sandra's suggestions were flawless, and Mikey found himself getting most of the bedroom and living room items – including a fabulous wooden king-sized bed with a brand new memory foam mattress.

As Sandra was ringing up his purchases at the sales counter, she appeared to be pondering something. Her face was scrunched up as if she were trying to concentrate on something.

"Is everything okay?" Mikey asked.

"Well, I hope you don't mind me asking, but are you gay?"

Mikey was taken aback. He quickly checked his outfit, wondering if he had accidentally wandered out of the house this morning wearing the rainbow booty shorts he wore to last year's Midsumma Festival. This was twice he'd been asked that question in a matter of hours. In Melbourne, no one ever asked him if he were gay. Maybe he stood out less in the city? Or perhaps he stood out more in the country? After meeting the Grinder Boys earlier, he felt more comfortable answering Sandra, since their presence alone clearly made being gay a non-issue in this town.

"Actually, I am," he replied cautiously.

"Are you single?"

"Well, yes. But..."

"Oh, wonderful!" Sandra squealed! "I could introduce you to my son. He's about your age. He keeps telling me he's not gay, but he does a lot of bodybuilding, so you never know!"

Mikey wasn't sure what to make of that. Aside from getting set up on a blind date with a guy who probably wasn't gay, he'd barely been in town for five minutes. Dating wasn't exactly top of his priorities at the moment. He needed to get his life together first.

"Um, that's very kind of you. But I'm sort of 'off the market' at the moment."

"Oh," Sandra deflated slightly, "Well, you can decide for yourself this afternoon. Travis will be the one delivering your furniture."

"How much is delivery?" Mikey asked as he fished out his wallet and pulled out his credit card.

"$50, or $70 if you want him to deliver everything with his shirt off."

"Sandra!" Mikey said, mildly scandalised, "That's outrageous!" he declared with no heat. He couldn't believe she was pimping her own son out. Mikey then considered the entertainment value in a bodybuilder delivering his furniture half-naked, and suddenly found the store getting a little warmer.

"Although," he clarified, "$70 is a very reasonable delivery fee..."

"I'll add it to the bill!" Sandra said with a chuckle as she ran the credit card through the machine. Mikey probably should feel guilty, but it had been a long time since he had a cheap thrill, and $20 was a small price to pay.

~

Mikey made his farewells to Sandra and went across the street to the Cooper's Landing General Store. About the same size as Harrison's, the general store appeared to be half supermarket, half discount department store. One side was dedicated to food and groceries, the other was filled with a wide assortment of household goods, kitchen items, homewares and random stuff. Mikey grabbed a trolley and decided to visit the non-food side first.

After twenty minutes, he had filled an entire shopping trolley with cutlery, crockery, a set of pots and pans, some basic ovenware, a toaster, an electric kettle and a cheap coffee machine. He would have to order the other household items online, but he had the basic creature comforts covered now. He left the trolley with Mrs Abernathy, the owner of the store. She was a gregarious lady in her seventies with coke-bottle glasses and blue-rinsed hair, whose eyes nearly bugged out of her head when she saw the volume of purchases Mikey was making. He quickly grabbed another trolley and filled it with food items from the grocery side of the store.

As Mrs Abernathy scanned his mountain of purchases, glee in her eyes, she casually quizzed him about how he was enjoying Cooper's Landing and if there was anything Mikey couldn't find in her shop.

Mikey didn't want to tell her that he needed a lot of items that she didn't stock, and was happy to buy them online, but he imagined a shop owner would probably not like that answer.

"I was hoping to find some art supplies, but I couldn't see any."

"Oh, we don't get much call for that stuff out here. I could probably order it in from Bushman's Pass if you know what you're looking for. It'll take a day or so to get here," she said, determined to make an extra sale.

"Let's get through all this first, then we'll see about any add-ons," Mikey said with a chuckle. Mrs Abernathy laughed too, but he could see she was disappointed at having lost a sale. This woman would have made a brilliant stock trader.

When everything was totalled up, Mikey handed over his credit card, but Mrs Abernathy froze.

"Oh, I'm sorry, dear. We're cash only," she said quietly, subtly pointing to a sign behind her that read 'CASH ONLY!' in bold type.

Mikey wasn't accustomed to carrying cash. He'd never even been in a shop that didn't take cards before. As embarrassment flooded his cheeks, Mrs Abernathy quickly added, "There's an ATM two doors down. I'll hold everything for you, Mikey dear."

Relief flooded Mikey, as he headed out the door toward the ATM. Two doors down, he found what used to be a combination bank and post office. These composite businesses were common in rural areas, as sadly was their slow march to extinction. This one had clearly been closed for several years. A faded, handwritten sign, taped to the inside of the glass entry doors, declared that the nearest post office and bank branch was in Bushman's Pass. However, the ATM was still fully functional. Mikey inserted his card, withdrew enough cash to cover his purchases, plus a little extra just in case, then quickly returned to the general store.

"So," Mrs Abernathy said as she packed up his purchases, "Are you gay, or what?"

Mikey looked around and saw a queue of locals waiting with their groceries, clearly all keen to find out the answer.

"Do I get a discount if I am?" Mikey said with a chuckle.

"No discounts!" Mrs Abernathy said sharply as if he had asked the old woman for a kidney. She pointed to another sign, this one saying 'NO DISCOUNTS!' in an even bolder type than the previous sign.

"Oh, well then, yes, I am gay."

"Fair enough, dear."

"Mind if I ask why you're interested?"

"Um," Mrs Abernathy faltered, clearly having not expected this question, "Er, well, um, it's, er, always good to know... about my customers. So I can anticipate your needs."

Mikey didn't believe a word of it but decided to let it go. The old woman was struggling to come up with an excuse for her non-sequitur question. He didn't know why the whole town was obsessed with his sexual orientation, but there didn't seem to be any hostility behind it.

He paid for his items and slowly loaded them into the SUV. By the time he was done, the vehicle looked almost as full as it had the previous day. Mikey took a moment to look for a local mechanic on Google. He found one, but it wouldn't be convenient to take the SUV in today, so he made an appointment for the following morning. Once the car was checked over and any repairs that it needed were complete. Mikey would need to find himself a more suitable vehicle. He knew that Cooper's Landing didn't have a car dealership. A town this small could never support such a huge business. Perhaps a trip out to Bushman's Pass in the next day or so was in order?

~

Once he had unloaded his shopping from the SUV into the living room, Mikey sat on the floor and started unpacking everything. Within an hour or so, the fridge and kitchen cupboards were full and the dish rack was filled with his freshly washed kitchenware. He looked at the time and realised that Travis would be there soon with his furniture.

Mikey headed to the main bedroom, where most of his stuff had been dumped the night before, so he could move his bags and various other items out of the way, giving Travis clear and easy access.

However, the moment he stepped into the room, something didn't feel right. He looked around, and everything seemed slightly off. As if each of the bags had been moved fractionally from their previous position.

Mikey examined one of the suitcases more closely and noticed that it had been opened and left slightly ajar. The suitcase contained personal documents and various paperwork. He hadn't had any reason to open it since he arrived, so there should be no reason why it shouldn't still be closed.

Mikey moved the bags out of the way into one of the spare bedrooms, then returned to the kitchen. It was then he noticed the glass sliding door that led out to the back porch wasn't closed properly. Mikey knew for a fact the door was closed and locked before he left the house that morning, and he hadn't had cause to open it since returning.

He quickly went around the house, looking to see if anything else looked out of place. Nothing was missing as far as he could tell. But then again, there wasn't much to steal. If he had been the victim of a burglar, the burglar must have walked away thoroughly disappointed.

Mikey then thought about how curious everyone in town had been about him. Everywhere he went, he was peppered with personal questions and queries about his life. Could that curiosity have actually spilt over to someone breaking into his house to get this inside scoop? Since his nearest neighbours were at least a mile away, and the ranch was so far off the beaten track, Mikey found it unlikely that anyone would be so desperate for gossip that they would go to such extraordinary lengths.

He reached for his phone intending to call the police, but then stopped himself. Was it really worth getting the police involved? Nothing was damaged or stolen. Nobody was hurt. It seemed almost a waste of time getting the boys in blue out here for such a trivial matter. Besides, it was almost certainly just a curious neighbour, Mikey reassured himself.

He was broken from his reverie by the sound of an approaching truck. Travis had arrived with the furniture. Mikey stepped out onto the porch in time to see a muscular young man climb out of the cab. His shirt was absent, and his well-toned physique glistened in the afternoon sun.

"You must be Mikey," the adonis said as he approached, "I'm Travis. Nice to meet you," he said with a wicked grin. Mikey was a little taken aback. Travis had to be almost ten years younger than him. Sandra was either paying him a compliment or expressing her serious need for corrective eye surgery when she said her son was about Mikey's age.

"Yes, nice to meet you too. I've cleared the way for you. I'll show you where I need everything to go."

Mikey quickly showed Travis around the house and the young man started to bring in the heavy furniture. Mikey almost offered to help, but it was clear that Travis took pride in his strength, or at least showing off how strong he was. Either way, Mikey didn't mind the show, even if it made him feel like a bit of a creeper now that he knew Travis couldn't be more than twenty years old.

When Travis was finished and everything was where he needed it to be, Mikey brought the younger man a chilled bottle of water. Travis cracked open the lid and began drinking it in almost slow motion, the cool water slowly spilling down his chin and across his muscular chest. Mikey nearly gasped at the sight, and Travis flashed that wicked grin again.

"Can I ask you something, Mikey?"

"Sure."

"How much did my mother charge you for me to take my shirt off?"

Mikey had just taken a sip of his own bottled water and immediately started choking on it. Travis came over and patted him on the back.

"It's okay, don't worry. I'm not mad. I'm just curious."

"Twenty bucks," Mikey admitted sheepishly.

"Seriously? She must have liked you. She charged Scott and Sean fifty."

Mikey burst out laughing. Sandra was absolutely diabolical! She must be desperate to get her son a boyfriend if she was will to use her business as an impromptu matchmaking service.

"I'm so sorry. I feel so creepy, paying to have you…"

"Oh don't worry about it. I like showing off my body," Travis said, demonstrating his lack of malice by openly posing and flexing his muscles.

"You don't mind your Mum…er…" Mikey tried to find a delicate way of putting it.

"Pimping me out?" Travis suggested. Mikey chuckled, nodding his agreement.

"Well, at least I know I've got some beer money waiting for me when I get home. Besides, I'm used to it. Ever since Mum got it into her head that I was gay, she's been on a mad quest to fix me up."

"But you're not gay, are you?"

"Nah. But don't spread it around. Ever since word got around that Mum was setting me up with men, I've had every girl in town trying to 'convert' me. It's been amazing!" he enthused.

"Well, that's awesome. I mean, officially, I'm offended, but I'm just glad you're happy," Mikey said. The two men laughed and finished their drinks in the afternoon sun.

~

After dinner and a quick shower, Mikey curled up on his new, super comfortable plush sofa in the living room and opened his laptop. He started ordering the remaining items he needed for around the house, mostly basic odds and ends and some art supplies so he could start painting as soon as possible. These items would most likely start showing up over the next week or so. In the meantime, the house was mostly livable, he could cook meals for himself and even have morning coffee. All in all, he'd done well in just twenty-four hours. The house was quickly turning into a home.

Once the online ordering was complete, Mikey placed the closed laptop on his new coffee table, turned out the lights and headed into the main bedroom. The massive bed was made and ready to sleep in, and that was exactly what Mikey intended to do. It had been a very long day, and he was ready to sink into that brand new mattress and let sleep take him. Within minutes, Mikey was blissfully nodding off, feeling more relaxed and content than ever before.

Chapter Four

IT HAD BEEN over a week since Wayne had encountered the cute city guy who had been stranded out on Dry Gully Road. Despite having been busy with assisting the narcotics task force in Bushman's Pass for the last four days, his thoughts had never wandered far from the handsome man with his overpriced lemon.

Wayne kept wondering how he was fairing in his new home. Was he adapting to country life? Had he heeded Wayne's advice and found himself a more reliable car? If Wayne asked him out on a date, would he say yes?

Now that he was back in Cooper's Landing and back to his normal routine, he might get a chance to catch up with Mikey and find out the answers to some of those questions. But one thing was nagging at the back of his mind that gave him pause. His mother.

Mavis, despite his objections, had promised to use her powers (or at the very least, her fellow gossips) to find out everything about Mikey and report back. So far, he hadn't heard a word from her. At all.

Ordinarily, Wayne would receive daily texts and voicemails from his mother; informing him on a wide variety of local topics, whether he wanted to get them or not. Everything from who had been seen visiting Mrs Tanner late at night while her husband was out of town, to the latest juicy details of Mr and Mrs Bentley's ugly divorce drama.

But ever since leaving for Bushman's Pass and his subsequent return, it was like Mavis Townsend had gone on radio silence. Wayne decided, since it was close enough to the end of the day, to drop around to her house and find out what was happening.

After checking in with Shirl at the station and making a brief pit stop at home to take a quick shower and change into some clean clothes, Wayne headed over to his mother's house. He pulled into her driveway just as the early evening shadows started casting their shapes across the front of his childhood home. The lights inside were on, and

Wayne could smell something delicious wafting through the open front door.

"Mum? It's me. Are ya decent?" Wayne called out as he stepped inside.

"Am I ever, dear?" Mavis shouted from the kitchen, cackling like a witch, "Come on in, dinner's almost ready."

Wayne didn't need to be told twice. As he entered the kitchen, he saw his mother by the stove stirring a big pot that could only be her Sausages in Brown Onion Gravy. Next to it were a couple of smaller pots containing vegetables and his mother's legendary mashed potatoes. He had picked the right night to visit.

"Set the table and sit yourself down while I plate everything up," Mavis said, as she whizzed back and forth, piling their plates high with delicious-looking food.

They immediately tucked into their dinner, and Wayne couldn't contain his sigh of contentment as he savoured his first mouthful. It had been ages since she had made this dish and it was one of Wayne's favourites. In the back of his mind, he suspected this may be a red flag, but was too distracted by his mother's buttery mashed potatoes to think about it at that moment.

"So," his mother said cautiously, "You've been quiet lately."

"Funny, I was going to say the same thing about you."

"Oh, well, I didn't want to disturb you when you were working with the narcotics task force. I figured they'd be keeping you busy."

"How did you know I was working with the narcotics task force?"

Mavis quirked an incredulous eyebrow at her son, "There's very little that happens in this town that I don't know about, kid."

"Shirl's been chinwagging again," Wayne muttered to himself, "I'll have to have a talk with her..."

"Now don't go getting her in trouble," his mother said softly, "She didn't give away any state secrets. She just mentioned you'd been asked to help out with the task force for a few days. Sounds exciting!"

"Sounds more exciting than it was. Four days of operating roadblocks and checking the backs of cars and trucks for drug shipments. It was basically highway patrol but slower. I was so glad to finally get back home."

"Well, maybe next time you'll get to have a car chase or blow something up," Mavis said with just a hint of sarcasm.

"Fingers crossed!" Wayne said enthusiastically.

"Wayne! That's a horrible thing to wish for!" Mavis scolded, "Is that really what you want?"

"Well, I wouldn't say no to a little excitement around here. Something more exciting than responding to complaints of funny smells on Beaumont Street."

"Mrs Patterson's casserole again?" Mavis said with a wry smile

"She was experimenting with her Apricot Chicken recipe," Wayne sighed, "We ended up having to bury it in her backyard."

Wayne tried to maintain a straight face, but when his mother burst out laughing, he couldn't help but join her. While his life in Cooper's Landing may not be all car chases and shootouts, it was certainly unique.

~

After dinner, Wayne and Mavis enjoyed a cold beer out on the front porch, watching as the stars appeared across the swirling opal sky. The cool evening breeze was a welcome change from the sticky humidity that Wayne had been suffering from all day.

"So," Wayne said, "I haven't heard anything from you regarding your secret mission."

Mavis flinched momentarily, but recovered quickly and took a sip of her beer, "What secret mission, dear?" she said, coyly.

Wayne just stared at her, blankly cocking an eyebrow at her. Over the years, he had learned that sometimes, when interrogating suspects, it was better not to say anything and let *them* fill the uncomfortable silence. It didn't take long for his mother to crack.

"Oh, alright! I didn't want to bring it up, because I didn't want to upset you."

"Upset me? What are you talking about?"

Mavis took another fortifying sip of her beer, placed the bottle down and folded her hands together.

"Well, I asked around town about your Mikey, and it turns out he *is* gay..."

"That's great!"

"But... he's already seeing someone."

Wayne felt himself deflate almost immediately. Of course, he was seeing someone. A gorgeous guy like Mikey wasn't going to be single. His boyfriend was probably finishing things up in Melbourne and would be joining Mikey in Cooper's Landing shortly.

"I'm sorry, darl," Mavis said comfortingly.

"Nah, it's okay. I figured he wouldn't be single. Any idea when the boyfriend will be showing up. You know, so I can litter his car with parking tickets?" Wayne said with an evil grin.

"That's horrible!" Mavis admonished, "Travis doesn't deserve that."

"Travis? As in Travis Harrison?"

"Yeah, apparently they met when Travis delivered some furniture to Mikey's house and now they're dating."

Wayne was beginning to suspect he was having some kind of stroke. None of this made any sense. Travis Harrison wasn't even gay. As far as he knew, he just pretended to be gay to get girls. Wayne had learned that the hard way a few months ago when his mother had set the two of them up on a blind date. It had been a disastrous evening, to say the least.

"Mum, Travis isn't gay. Where are you getting this rubbish from?"

"Sandra! She's the one who said he was gay and that Mikey was going out with him!" Mavis said, defending her sources.

"Well, I hate to break it to you, but Sandra is 100% wrong. Travis is straight. Which means your gossip reliability quotient just plummeted."

Mavis looked like she had just swallowed a very bitter lemon, "Just you wait until I get my hands on Sandra Harrison..."

"Don't you say a word about it! Travis is apparently quite happy with everyone thinking he's gay. He reckons all the local girls want to 'convert' him, and he has no complaints with them making attempts."

"That's disgraceful!" his mother said indignantly, "Although, since you have something to hold over his head, you can blackmail him for sex!"

"Mother!" Wayne said, genuinely shocked at such a suggestion.

"What?" she said innocently.

"Aside from the fact that Travis is over a decade younger than me, I think you'll find *blackmail* is illegal!"

"Yeah, I suppose... that being said, have you seen him without his shirt off? Best twenty bucks I ever spent!"

"What?!"

"Oh, nothing dear," Mavis said, absently staring at the antique stone birdbath in the front yard, a shy smile curling on her lips.

"I'm going to pretend I didn't hear any of that."

So, Mikey is gay *and* possibly single. Wayne was still in with a shot. Now all he needed was to bump into him in town at some point. But that could take days to happen naturally. He needed to come up with some excuse to visit Mikey directly. But what reason would the local police sergeant have for visiting the man's home?

~

The next morning, Wayne was exhausted. He had tossed and turned for most of the night, trying to come up with a seemingly legitimate reason to visit Mikey. The best thing he could come up with was conducting a security audit, but he couldn't come up with a legitimate reason to do it. There hadn't been any break-ins in the area. He'd have to think of something soon.

Too tired to make himself breakfast, Wayne decided to head into town early and grab something at the coffee shop. The Grinder Boys had become very popular in the town since it had opened a few years earlier. Their 'trucker's breakfast' and coffee was just what he needed to shake away the cobwebs and get his heart started.

Arriving at the cafe, the place was packed. Sean and Scott looked like they were being run off their feet, juggling multiple orders. Wayne gave Sean the nod, indicating that he'd like his usual order, and Sean nodded back in acknowledgement. Wayne then sat down at the last empty table and awaited his breakfast.

As he began reading the local newspaper and sipping his coffee, Wayne noticed a shiny new ute pull up outside the cafe. The pickup truck-style utility vehicle, commonly driven by tradesmen and people in rural areas, didn't stand out amongst the others parked nearby, except for its driver. Wayne nearly choked on his coffee when he saw Mikey emerge from the ute. But he was instantly relieved that the city boy had taken his advice and found himself a more suitable vehicle.

Mikey strode into the cafe wearing a nice pair of crisp blue jeans, a white t-shirt and a sturdy pair of work boots, headed straight to the counter and ordered 'the usual' from Sean with a grin. Wayne smiled at the transformation in their little town's newest resident in just one week. By this time next month, he'd be indistinguishable from a born and bred local.

The cute city boy looked around for a free table, but the cafe was still packed. Wayne, keen for an opportunity to talk to Mikey, carefully pushed the spare chair at his table out in invitation.

"Room for one more here," Wayne said with a smile.

"Oh, thank you, Sergeant. You're too kind," Mikey said, returning his smile and taking a seat.

"Don't mention it, and call me Wayne. You only need to call me Sergeant if I'm arresting you."

"In that case, I'll keep my illegal activities firmly under wraps until after breakfast," Mikey said, glancing toward Scott, who was approaching with Wayne's breakfast.

As the gruff man placed the huge plate down in front of Wayne, Mikey's eyes went as wide as saucers.

"What?"

"That's your breakfast?"

"It's the Trucker's Special."

"Are you a trucker?"

"No, but I had a rough night, and occasionally I like to indulge in a big breakfast. Besides, I'm a growing boy!" Wayne smirked and playfully flexed his arms. He didn't miss how Mikey seemed to shiver all over at his display.

Scott interrupted the moment by bringing over a croissant and a cup of very strong looking coffee for Mikey. Wayne was taken aback. Such a small meal compared to his own. He wondered if Mikey was having trouble affording a proper breakfast. Wayne looked down at his enormous platter of food and suddenly felt ashamed at his greed. Here he was, pigging out on this insanely large meal, while Mikey could only afford coffee and a pastry.

"Are you sure you want to drink this? It's not healthy." Scott said sternly, holding the coffee just out of Mikey's reach. Mikey responded by frowning and making whimpering noises, like a puppy being denied a treat.

"You are a hopeless addict, boy. If you were mine, I'd beat it out of you and make you drink herbal tea!" Scott said gruffly as he reluctantly placed the coffee down on the table.

Mikey responded by barking happily and panting. Scott scowled, shook his head, but couldn't hide his smirk as he returned to the kitchen.

"What was that all about?" Wayne asked.

"He thinks I drink too much coffee. A weird complaint from a guy who owns a coffee shop. Speaking of which..." Mikey picked up the coffee and took a huge sip. The groan of appreciation he emitted made Wayne's trousers suddenly feel too tight.

Mikey began tucking into his little croissant and, again, Wayne felt guilty about his huge meal.

"Here, have some of my bacon. A pastry and some coffee isn't a proper breakfast."

Mikey chuckled, "You're as bad those two!" he pointed toward Scott and Sean as they continued to work steadily behind the counter, "They're constantly complaining that I need a 'real man's breakfast' or I'll waste away to nothing."

"Well, you will!"

"Nonsense. I'm not a big eater first thing in the morning. Never have been. I tried eating cooked breakfasts for a while, but it always made me feel queasy. I prefer something light. Well, light with a giant dose of caffeine."

"Addict!" Scott called from across the cafe, his bat-like hearing on full display. Mikey barked again and Scott scowled in reply.

Wayne was relieved that Mikey wasn't starving himself and that he apparently could afford a decent meal if he wanted one. The two men settled into eating their meals, exchanging pleasant small talk as they did.

Before long, Mikey had finished and was ready to leave. Wayne hadn't had a chance to ask him out, or even put the feelers out to find out if he would be interested in being asked out. He tried to think of something to say, but in a moment of panic, Wayne had nothing.

"Well, thanks for letting me share your table. I'll see you around, I guess." Mikey said as he got up to leave. Wayne wished him a good day and watched as the other man walked out of the cafe.

"He's a little cutie, isn't he?" Sean said, suddenly standing next to Wayne, gathering up Mikey's plate and cup. Wayne just nodded in reply

"Well, why didn't you ask him out?"

"I tried, but I suddenly didn't know what to say. Besides, he's from the city. I'm just a small-town cop. What would we have in common?"

"You mean, besides, your mutual attraction?" Sean said slyly.

Wayne was surprised. Did Mikey really like him? If so, what was he going to do about it? He didn't have time to worry about it now, he needed to get to work soon. He had promised Shirl he would finish off his highway patrol reports today so she could send them off and file them away. Wayne quickly finished his breakfast and coffee, then headed off to the station.

Chapter Five

MIKEY'S FIRST WEEK in Cooper's Landing had certainly kept him busy. Between ordering furniture, setting up his new home and his trip to Bushman's Pass to replace his vehicle, he had barely had a moment to relax. As he drove back to the ranch after breakfast, his thoughts turned to Wayne. With all his dashing around, Mikey hadn't had the opportunity to run into the hunky country cop since the day he arrived in town.

Wayne hadn't been far from Mikey's thoughts during the past week, especially when he was researching and eventually purchasing his new ute. Mikey had never pictured himself in such a vehicle. But the moment he sat behind the wheel, something just felt right. The cabin was spacious like his old SUV, and the back tray was more than large enough for his needs. More importantly, the ute was perfectly suited to unsealed country roads and harsh rural conditions. Breaking down in the middle of nowhere was one less thing to worry about.

So when Mikey walked into Grinder Boys for breakfast that day, he was pleasantly surprised to have the handsome police officer offer to share his table. Although their conversation had been brief and not especially in-depth, Mikey suspected Wayne wanted to say something more. He figured that perhaps the fact the cafe was so busy had put Wayne off from a more intimate discussion.

Mikey shook his head. Like Wayne would have any interest in a man like him. Wayne was a country boy through and through. He'd probably want someone from a similar background. Someone rough and tumble with strong farmer's muscles. Someone he could go hunting or fishing with. Not a city guy with a head for numbers and a love of painting. And painting was all he could think about right now.

As Mikey pulled up outside the ranch, he couldn't contain his excitement. For today would be Mikey's first day of 'work' – his first full day as an artist. Mikey went inside, assembled his equipment and supplies, and began setting up on the wide back porch that overlooked the rest of the property.

Mikey couldn't have picked a better day to start his new artistic life. The sun was warm but not too hot; the clear blue sky was bright and vibrant and there was a gentle, cool breeze that brought with it a light scent of wildflowers from the nearby paddocks.

The view from the back porch was nothing short of spectacular. On the far horizon was the green, tree-filled hills of the neighbouring national park. This represented the northern boundary of Mikey's property. Between that and the main ranch house was a field of unkempt grazing land that, once upon a time, had been neatly fenced off into separate paddocks. Now they were overgrown with long grass and wildflowers, separated only by the disintegrating remains of wooden fenceposts and broken fallen gates.

Directly behind the main house was what remained of the ranch's original outer buildings. The previous owners had only bothered to renovate the main house and left the outer buildings untouched, correctly surmising that anyone who wanted to buy the property would either want to replace or simply demolish the ageing structures. To the right was a large wooden barn. It would have been an impressive structure in its day, but had now fallen into disrepair; it's flaking, faded paint retaining only an afterimage of the reverberant red and white colours of its operational years. Mikey had inspected the barn a few days earlier but determined it was not safe to enter. He could see from the outside that the barn was filled with half a century of junk and disused farm equipment. Nothing of value or worthy of salvage.

To the left was the old bunkhouse and stables. Like the barn, these buildings were also succumbing to the ravages of time. The wooden structures were falling apart and no longer fit for habitation. Mikey intended to have the outer buildings demolished once he had settled in. But before he did, he wanted to capture their likenesses for posterity.

Mikey set up his easel, prepared a large canvas and arranged the set of oil paints and brushes that had arrived in the mail yesterday. It had been quite some time since he had last painted anything, but the moment his brush made contact with the canvas, it was like no time had passed at all. If there had been any doubts in Mikey's mind about whether his move to Cooper's Landing had been the right choice; about leaving his fast-paced city life behind to follow his bliss in the country, then those doubts were quickly erased as he slowly but surely filled the canvas with colour, shapes and brushstrokes. As he took his time reproducing on the canvas what he saw in front of him, Mikey finally felt like he was home. No more living up to his father's expectations. No more working in a boring, soul-destroying job he hated. Just the canvas, the paint and the unending horizon. This was definitely his bliss.

~

Before he knew it, the day had flowed away and all he had done was paint. He looked at his watch and realised it was approaching five in the afternoon. Mikey was hesitant to stop painting, but he was losing the light and he had to admit, he was getting seriously hungry since he had completely skipped lunch. Mikey quickly packed up his art supplies, carefully transferred everything including the canvas to the spare room he now thought of as his 'Art Studio,' and headed to the bathroom to wash up.

By the time he had finished showering and dressing into some comfortable clothes, the sun had set and the stars were starting to appear in the inky black night sky. Mikey entered the kitchen and prepared himself a simple omelette and salad for dinner. He sat down and enjoyed his meal at his new kitchen table.

Afterwards, he went to the kitchen sink and began washing up the dishes. As he absently dried the plates and cutlery, he stared out the kitchen window, taking in the view of his property. He still couldn't believe how different the night sky looked compared to the city. Without the light pollution of the sprawling metropolis, the sky was free to reveal its majestic beauty. The swirling clouds of stars and galaxies filled the sky from horizon to horizon.

As he dried the last plate, Mikey noticed something moving outside in the distance. Lights. Dull and far away; moving erratically; almost like fireflies. Of course, there were no fireflies in this part of Australia. The lights moved and weaved close to the northern boundary. They were fading away, almost as if they were going into the national park. Mikey had no idea what they were.

He was interrupted from his thoughts by a sharp knocking on his front door. Mikey dried his hands on the dishtowel, walked into the living room and opened the front door to reveal Wayne in full police uniform.

"Hi," Mikey said with a smile, "I wasn't expecting you. Would you like to come in?"

Wayne looked nervous, but nodded and came in, removing his hat as he entered.

"Is something wrong?" Mikey asked, beginning to wonder if this was an official visit.

"Oh, no. I just finished work and I thought I might drop around and see how you were settling in."

"Well, it's all coming together really well, as you can see. Would you like a little tour?" Mikey said.

Wayne smiled and nodded as Mikey led his visitor around the house, pointing out his new furniture and eventually showing off the canvas he had been working on that day.

"Ahhh, so this is what you do for a living..." Wayne said as he examined the unfinished painting, "Your work is exceptional. You have a real gift."

"Thank you, but I'm not sure it counts as a 'living' as such. Technically I'm unemployed. My painting is mostly for my enjoyment, not my job."

Wayne seemed a little confused by this statement, but Mikey decided to leave any further explanations for the moment. He didn't want to say outright that he was cashed up and didn't need a job. Mikey didn't want to sound like he was bragging or rubbing his wealth in anyone's face.

When they reached the kitchen, Mikey offered to make Wayne a cup of coffee.

"No thanks, it'll keep me awake all night," Wayne said stiffly. Mikey couldn't help but notice that Wayne was looking pensive, much as he had that morning at breakfast.

"Is everything okay?" Mikey asked carefully.

"Yeah. It's just... Well... I was thinking of asking you out... to dinner... you know... with me?"

"Oh, I see," Mikey chuckled, "Well if it makes it easier for you, I would probably say yes."

"Mikey, would you like to..."

"Yes!"

The two men laughed. Wayne's whole body visibly relaxed immediately and his face bore a wide smile.

"Really? You'll go out with me?"

"Sure. I just had dinner, but I'm free tomorrow night."

"I'll pick you up at seven. Well, I should probably go. I need to get some sleep. Busy day tomorrow." the police officer said, unable to wipe the grin off his face. Mikey escorted him to the door and waved him goodbye as Wayne drove off down the dusty road into the darkness of the evening.

A perfect end to a perfect day. Mikey had a feeling Cooper's Landing was just what his life had been missing.

Chapter Six

THE NEXT DAY, Wayne was walking on cloud nine. The sun was shining brighter than usual; the sounds of birdsong were extra sweet; his morning coffee had tasted better than ever and, oh yes, Mikey had said 'yes' to him! He tried not to get ahead of himself, but Wayne couldn't help but feel excited.

That evening, Wayne would be taking Mikey out on their first official date. Okay, it wasn't going to be anything too fancy. Cooper's Landing didn't offer a wide variety of options when it came to date venues. It was either dinner at the town diner or drive all the way to Bushman's Pass for the night. He briefly considered taking Mikey to the pub for the evening, but they only served snacks and the loud atmosphere wouldn't be great for getting to know each other. Wayne decided the diner was the best choice. The food was decent and the diner had a casual, relaxed atmosphere.

Ever since he had met the cute city boy a week or so ago, Wayne had felt a spark between them. It wasn't just simple attraction or infatuation. Wayne had been attracted to plenty of guys before. But Mikey was different. He felt special. Wayne wasn't sure what it was that made the city boy different, only that he couldn't get him out of his mind, and that every time Mikey smiled at him, it made his stomach flip.

After a quiet morning on highway patrol, Wayne decided to drop in on his Mum, who had insisted he make an appearance for lunch. He half expected to arrive to the aroma of roast beef with all the trimmings, suspecting Mavis was up to something again. However, when he pulled into her driveway and got out of his car, all Wayne could smell was the floral scent of his mother's carefully manicured flower beds.

Wayne found his mother in the kitchen, busying herself making sandwiches and putting the finishing touches on a big bowl of potato salad (with extra paprika sprinkled on top – just the way Wayne liked it) signalling that Mavis was indeed up to something, and he had a strong suspicion what it was.

"Hi, Mum. Have you been behaving yourself?"

"Of course!" Mavis replied, placing the bowl of potato salad on the kitchen table and silently inviting her son to sit down and help himself to food. Wayne sat down, casting a suspicious eye over his mother briefly, then started to dish out some potato salad onto his plate.

"So," Mavis said casually, "How are things going?"

"Well," Wayne said, equally casually, "things are going fine."

Mavis narrowed her eyes, clearly unsatisfied with her son's vague response. She tried again, this time with a little less subtlety, "And what about Mikey? How is he going?"

"Things are going fine for Mikey too," Wayne smirked.

His mother scowled. Wayne was having a hard time not laughing out loud at her incredulity. He had correctly guessed this little lunch meeting was in aid of his mother getting the latest gossip on her son's love life. He briefly considered playing dumb but decided to put his mother out of her misery and come clean.

"I asked him out on a date and he said yes."

"Oh, darling! That's wonderful! I knew you'd catch him in the end!" Mavis practically squealed with delight. Wayne needed to shut this down before his mother got too ahead of herself.

"Okay, calm down! It's just a date. For all we know, we have nothing in common and it will be a total disaster."

"Rubbish! You need to think more positively, darling. If you walking into this date thinking it will be a disaster, of course, it will be."

"I'm just saying, don't get too excited. Don't start planning any weddings or anything."

"Alright, alright. I promise to keep expectations low. Now, tell me everything. When is the date? Where are you going? What are you going to wear?" Mavis enthused, clearly pumping him for information.

Wayne wasn't a fool. The last thing he needed was his mother showing up while he and Mikey were trying to enjoy their evening together. Mavis had a history of dropping in 'coincidentally' on a number of his blind dates over the years, much to Wayne's chagrin.

"No way! No more details. The only people who need to know about the date are me and Mikey." Wayne said, adopting his hard-as-nails cop facade. Mavis was clearly disappointed but must have realised she wasn't going to strong-arm her son out of any information he didn't want to divulge.

As Wayne helped himself to another plateful of potato salad, his phone began ringing.

"Darling, how many times do I have to tell you. No phones at the dinner table?" she gently admonished.

"Sorry Mum, but I'm on duty," Wayne said as he answered the phone.

"Cooper's Landing Police, Sgt Townsend speaking."

"Wayne, it's me," Old Shirl replied, "That new guy in town? The one from the old Riverside Ranch? He just called in a disturbance at his property. There's apparently been some damage."

Wayne's blood went cold as ice.

Mikey.

"What are the details?"

"Someone threw a rock through one of his windows. He claims there was a threatening note attached."

"I'm on my way now. ETA is ten minutes." Wayne said briskly, hanging up and standing to leave.

"Sorry Mum, duty calls. There's trouble out at Mikey's place. I have to go. Thanks for lunch," he said, quickly giving his mother a kiss on the cheek.

"I hope everything is okay, darling. Call me later, so I don't worry."

"I promise."

Wayne strode out to the car and made his way directly to Mikey's house, using the lights and sirens as required to clear the minimal traffic out of his way. When he arrived at the Riverside Ranch, Mikey was standing on the porch, his arms wrapped around himself, his tension and stress evident. The large front window next to him had been smashed. Wayne got out of the car and was pleased to see Mikey visibly relax as he approached.

"Are you okay? Are you hurt?"

"No, no I'm fine. Just a little shaken up."

"What happened?"

Mikey escorted him inside to the living room. The floor was covered with jagged shards of broken glass.

"I was out the back, doing some painting when I suddenly heard the window smash. When I came in, I found this," he said, pointing to the living room floor. Amongst the broken glass was a large rock and a crumpled piece of paper.

"I picked it up and took the note off. I probably shouldn't have done that, but I wasn't thinking straight. I hope I haven't ruined it for fingerprints."

"That's okay, don't worry about it," Wayne reassured him, "I think anyone would have done the same thing." He pulled out a pair of latex gloves from his trouser pocket, put them on, and carefully picked up the note by one corner, trying to avoid contaminating the note further.

The note was written on a piece of standard notepad paper. Nothing fancy or distinctive. The words 'GO HOME FAG' were crudely scrawled in black ink.

Wayne was shocked. This kind of homophobia was well and truly a thing of the past in Cooper's Landing. At least, it should be. He hadn't seen anything like this in over a decade. Not since the incident with Sammy Hansen and the disgraceful treatment he received at the hands of the local police at the time. After everything that happened to Sammy, Cooper's Landing had made a point of moving beyond such backwards attitudes and had, over the subsequent years, welcomed many LGBTQ people into the local community.

"Have you had any other homophobic interactions since you arrived in town?"

"No. Nothing. In fact, I was genuinely surprised at how accepting and welcoming everyone has been. You hear a lot of horror stories about country towns..."

"Cooper's Landing isn't like other country towns. We don't want a repeat of what happened a few years ago." Wayne said, examining the rock.

"What happened?" Mikey asked.

"Have you noticed anything unusual around here or perhaps when you've been in town?" Wayne asked, disregarding Mikey's question. He needed to establish all the facts while they were fresh in Mikey's mind. He could fill him in on town history later. "Maybe someone following you or watching you?"

"The whole town's been watching me since day one, but I can't think of anything..." Mikey paused mid-sentence as if remembering something.

"Mikey?"

"I wasn't going to say anything. I dismissed it at the time. The second day I was here, I could have sworn somebody had been in the house while I was out. Some stuff had been moved around like they had been searching through my bags. And the back door was unlocked when I got home when I was certain I locked it before going out."

"Why didn't you report this?"

"I thought perhaps it was just a nosy neighbour, wanting to get a scoop on the new guy in town. Plus, nothing was damaged or missing, so it seemed like a waste of time calling the police in. Besides, maybe I did forget to lock the back door? I don't know. But now with this incident, I don't know what to think."

Wayne could understand the curiosity of the people of Cooper's Landing. But he found it highly unlikely that even the most hardcore of the town gossips would go to the extent of trespassing on private property just to snoop on the new guy in town. He examined the back door. The lock on the sliding glass door was cheap and easy to get past.

"I would strongly recommend getting a locksmith in ASAP to change all the locks. These locks aren't exactly the best quality and could be easily picked. There's a good locksmith in Bushman's Pass that I can give you the number for."

"Is that really necessary? I thought the good thing about country towns was that nobody had to lock their doors, let alone have super strong locks on the doors?"

Wayne chuckled, "That was decades ago. The days of leaving the doors unlocked and the car keys in the ignition are long gone. Crime is way lower out here than in the city, but it still happens from time to time. So it's best to take precautions."

"Okay, I'll give the locksmith a ring. Right after I sort out a glazier to sort out this window," Mikey said, looking a lot more confident than before.

"In the meantime, I'd secure the sliding doors and windows with some dowelling or something solid and sturdy when going out. An old broom handle would do for the sliding door. I'm sure you can find some suitable materials scattered around outside. Right now, I'll grab some evidence bags out of the car and bag up the rock and note. I'll get the locksmith's number for you while I'm at it."

"Thanks, Wayne. I'll start making some calls. Hopefully, I can get the window done soon."

After taking some photos of the scene, collecting the evidence and helping to sweep up the broken glass, Wayne was finished and ready to go.

"I better get moving. I need to make some enquiries around town. See if anyone knows anything or has overheard any homophobic stuff recently," Wayne said as he headed outside with Mikey.

"Thanks again for coming out so quickly," Mikey said, looking a little crestfallen, "Look, I know we were supposed to be going out tonight, but would you mind if we took a raincheck? After all this, I'm not really in a going out kind of mood. Besides, I have no idea how long it's going to take for the glazier to show up."

"Of course. That's no problem. I'm going to be busy writing up reports on all this anyway. We'll have dinner another night. Take care and don't hesitate to call me if you need anything."

"Before you go," Mikey said, looking hesitant, "Earlier you said about something like this happening years ago. What were you going to say?"

Wayne sighed. He wished he hadn't mentioned it. The last thing he wanted to do was frighten or upset Mikey any further, but he'd likely find out from someone in town eventually. Better it came from him than some random gossip.

"A few years ago, before I joined the force, there was an incident here in Cooper's Landing."

"An incident?"

"A young guy named Sammy. He was openly gay and, for the most part, the town was very accepting."

"But?"

"He found himself the victim of a stalker. A guy he went out on a single date with. The guy became obsessed with Sammy. It started harmlessly enough, but the guy quickly became abusive and it scared the hell out of Sammy. He went to the police but, at the time, Cooper's Landing Police was staffed by a bunch of self-righteous homophobic pricks. They dismissed Sammy's concerns, and even went as far as threatening to charge him with wasting police time."

"That's horrible," Mikey said, "So, what happened?"

"The stalker attacked Sammy. Broke into his house in the middle of the night and..." Wayne cut himself off. "Sammy survived, but he was in the hospital for months afterwards."

"And the stalker?"

"Disappeared without a trace. When it got out that the police knew about the threats against Sammy and did absolutely nothing, the whole town was outraged. The mayor demanded an inquiry and eventually, the whole station was dismissed. My old Sargent, the man who recruited me into the force, ended up moving here from Bushman's Pass to take over the station."

"Does Sammy still live here in town?" Mikey asked, his voice barely a whisper.

"Sadly, no. After he came home from the hospital, he started getting threatening messages again. Unable to trust the police to protect him, he ended up packing his bags and disappearing one night. Didn't tell anyone he was planning on moving. He sold his house and left a note on the front door saying something vague about getting a job offer out of town. He was listed as a missing person until a couple of years ago."

"He was found?"

"Yes. Turns out he changed his name, moved to Melbourne and was living in hiding. I only found out when a detective from Melbourne called the station asking about Sammy's case file. He's safe and well, living a new life."

"I'm glad he's okay, but that's a horrifying story." Mikey looked like he was terrified out of his mind. Wayne felt like a total shit. He should have just shut his mouth.

"I'm sorry. I shouldn't have dumped all that on you. It's probably the last thing you need right now."

"It's fine. I'm fine. I promise." Mikey didn't sound like he was fine, but he was putting on a brave front.

"Hey," Wayne put his hands on Mikey's shoulder, giving them a gentle squeeze, "This isn't the same thing. I promise I'll get to the bottom of this. Chances are, this is just some run of the mill homophobe who's too much of a coward for a direct confrontation, so they do something stupid like this." Wayne gestured to the broken window.

Mikey seemed to relax, and he looked up at Wayne with a shy smile. The look gave Wayne a sort of fluttering feeling deep in his chest. The younger man was gorgeous.

"Okay, I need to get back to the station. Call me anytime, day or night, if you need anything or if something doesn't feel right."

Mikey nodded and Wayne let go of his shoulders, turned away and got in the car. As he drove away, Wayne looked back at the city boy in the rear vision mirror. Mikey was standing on the porch, watching him back.

"I'll find whoever did this," Wayne muttered to himself, "Whatever it takes."

Chapter Seven

AS MIKEY STOOD on the front porch, watching Wayne slowly drove away, he tried to maintain his composure. Although Wayne's arrival had initially settled his nerves, now that the police officer had left, he was left feeling very much alone and isolated on his remote property.

Mikey wasn't a fool. When he moved to a country town from the city, he hadn't expected his sexual identity to be universally supported. But he had to admit, the overwhelmingly positive reception he had received in his first few days in town had clearly left him with a false sense of security.

This incident had been a rude awakening.

Obviously, someone in town wasn't as accepting as the other residents of Cooper's Landing appeared to be. The fact that this person would go out of their way to come to his isolated house, break a window and deliver their hateful message, was creepy, to say the least.

Mikey had no close neighbours and he didn't recall hearing a car drive off after the window was broken, so the vandal must have been on foot, or possibly hidden their car far enough away for it not to be seen or heard by Mikey. Again, they seemed to have gone to a lot of trouble just to indulge in their bigotry. Something just didn't feel right about this incident, but Mikey couldn't quite put his finger on what.

Taking Wayne's advice, Mikey used some broom handles and old wood scraps to secure the windows and sliding doors from anyone attempting to open them from the outside. It would do until the locksmith arrived to upgrade the locks

A few hours later, the glazier from Bushman's Pass had finished replacing the broken window and everything was as good as new. No harm, no foul. However, shortly after the glazier left, the locksmith called to inform Mikey that he would unfortunately not be able to come out until the following afternoon. Although the property was reasonably secure now, Mikey still felt uneasy spending the night in the house until the locks had been properly secured. He knew it was irrational, but he just didn't want to be alone.

This situation had illustrated for the first time just how alone he really was in Cooper's Landing. Living on an isolated property, in a small country town where he barely knew anyone. No family or friends locally to turn to for support. His only real option was to get himself a room at the pub for the night.

The Royal Hotel on Main Street offered rooms above the main bar of the pub. While not ideal, at least Mikey could get a hot meal and a bed for the night. Tomorrow, he would deal with the locksmith, then he could feel safe in his own home again. He quickly packed an overnight bag with everything he would need, then headed out to his car.

~

Before heading to the hotel, Mikey decided to drop in on the Grinder Boys for a quick coffee. It was almost four pm and too early to be cooped up in a hotel room. Besides, after everything that had happened that day, he could use a caffeine hit to boost his seriously flagging energy levels.

Pulling up to the cafe, Mikey noticed all the outdoor tables and chairs had been packed away, leading him to suspect the boys must be getting ready to close up for the day. He hoped he could pop in quickly to get a last-minute takeaway cuppa, knowing the pub was unlikely to provide coffee of a decent quality. Entering, he saw Sean and Scott wiping down the inside tables. The cafe was devoid of customers.

"Heya, Mikey!" Sean said, abandoning his table wiping and approaching to greet him, "We were just closing up. What do you need?"

In that moment, Mikey was suddenly hit with the enormity of what had happened to him today. He had tried to push back his feelings of anger, frustration, violation and fear. But standing before these two men, who had been nothing but kind to him from the moment he arrived in town, he struggled to keep his composure. He felt a single tear run down his cheek and quickly wiped it away, hoping they hadn't noticed.

"Hey, hey, hey," Sean said soothingly, "What's happened? Talk to us." Scott dropped his dishrag and strode over to join them.

"I could really use a cup of coffee..." Mikey said, his voice barely a whisper.

"One triple shot latte, coming right up," Sean said, reaching out and giving Mikey's shoulder a reassuring squeeze before heading over to the coffee machine. Scott gave him a quick, gruff hug then guided him over to a table, setting up the chairs that had been stacked up on top of it.

"What's wrong? Has something happened?" Scott asked, his face etched with concern.

Mikey explained about the broken window and having to call Wayne out to his house, waiting for the glazier to arrive and the delay with the locksmith. Sean brought over his latte and Mikey took a long, fortifying sip. By the time he had explained about the homophobic note attached to the rock, Scott was growling with anger. Sean touched his partner's arm to calm him, but the big man was furious that someone would do this. He stood up and came over to examine Mikey up close.

"Are you hurt, boy?"

"No, not physically. I'm just a bit shaken up by the whole thing."

"Well, you just give me the name, boy. I'll take care of the rest." Scott said, brooking no argument.

"I don't know who did it. It all happened so fast, I didn't even see them. Besides, Wayne's on the case. He'll figure it out."

"And you shouldn't be going off half-cocked and taking the law into your own hands!" Sean gently admonished his partner. Scott scowled at him, but Sean just stared back at him. Eventually, Scott took a deep breath and seemed to visibly relax.

"I never do anything 'half-cocked'..." Scott grumbled. Sean smirked at him affectionately.

Oddly, Mikey was immediately reassured by Scott's bombastic reaction. It seemed he had made a couple of friends in town already without even realising. Maybe he wasn't so alone out here after all.

"Well, my house will be fully secured once the locksmith gets here tomorrow. Until then, I don't want to be there on my own, so I'm going to get a room at the pub for the night and..."

"Like hell, you will!" Scott boomed with outrage, his relaxed mood dissolving in seconds, "I won't hear of you staying in that rat-trap shithole!"

"I agree," Sean said, "That place is a dump. You'll come and spend the night at our place."

"Oh, I couldn't impose on you like that..."

"Nonsense, we insist," Scott said, "We have a nice guest room, we'll make dinner and then you can jump in our hot tub. It'll melt away all the stress of today. By the time your head hits the pillow, you'll be relaxed and ready for a good night's sleep. Yes, that's settled. You're coming home with us. No arguments, boy."

"Yes, sir!" Mikey said softly, smiling like an idiot. He was lucky to have such kind, generous friends. He quickly finished his coffee and the boys packed up the table set.

"Here!" Scott said gruffly, handing Mikey a broom, "You can sweep up the floor. The sooner we're done here, the sooner we can close and go home."

"No such thing as a free dinner, huh?" Mikey said cheekily.

"You got that right, boy!" Scott said, his booming laugh echoing around the empty cafe. Mikey laughed too and began sweeping the floor. A little manual labour was a small price to pay for dinner, a bed for a night and, most importantly, two charming new friends who had his back.

~

Sean and Scott lived in a cute little riverside cottage on the south side of town. While the exterior was typical of the other houses in the area, complete with carefully manicured rose bushes and ornamental hedges, the interior was very different. Upon entering the cosy living room, Mikey was confronted by an eclectic clash of interior design styles. Sort of a traditional English tea room combined with a BDSM sex club. A large black leather sofa with glass and chrome side tables was accented by delicate white lace doilies and matching ceramic candy dishes filled with potpourri. It was like visiting his grandmother's house – if his grandmother had been a Dominatrix.

"Make yourself at home, boy," Scott said, "I'll go and get dinner started."

"Are you sure I can't help you?" Mikey asked, not wanting to be any more of a burden than he already was.

"Nonsense! You're our guest. I wouldn't hear of it." Sean said as he followed his partner out of the room towards the back of the house.

Mikey looked around the living room, admiring the unusual décor choices. Classic flowery wallpaper and black and white erotic photography was a slightly avant-garde choice, but it suited his hosts perfectly. On the mantlepiece was a single silver frame. The photo was of Scott and Sean, standing with a third man – a younger, slim gentleman with beautiful shoulder-length blonde hair. The three men were clearly in a BDSM club, all dressed in leather, smiling and embracing in a three-way hug.

"That's Luke. He was our submissive for eight years." Sean said softly from the doorway.

"Oh, I'm sorry. I didn't mean to intrude," Mikey said, blushing at having been caught staring at the intimate photo.

"Not at all. I think you'll find we're pretty open about most things."

"Where is Luke now?"

Sean took a moment to respond as if steadying himself.

"Luke passed away from cancer a few years ago. It came out of nowhere and before we knew what was happening, he was gone."

"I'm so sorry, Sean. That must have been horrible." Mikey couldn't imagine the pain these two kind men must have been through.

"It was tough. It was also the reason Scott and I moved out here. We needed a change of scene. We still grieve for him, probably always will, but we've managed to move on. He's still with us, in our hearts."

Mikey crossed the room and gave Sean a big hug. Clearly, the man had not been expecting this, as he was a little stunned at first, but eventually relaxed and embraced him in a tight bear hug. He wondered idly if the boys would ever take on another sub, or if their BDSM days were really behind them. He would never be so bold as to ask, though. It was none of his business after all.

"So," Mikey said as he released Sean, "What's for dinner?"

"Scott said something about 'Beef Surprise' so it's anyone's guess. I'm sure it will be delicious though, it always is!"

"It's funny, Scott doesn't strike me as the cooking type."

"Well, behave yourself, boy, and we won't have to strike you at all!" Scott bellowed from the kitchen.

"Well, where's the fun in that?" Mikey said, waggling his eyebrows cheekily at Sean. The older man suppressed a chuckle, while Scott growled playfully from the other room.

Mikey couldn't hold back his laugh. He never thought in a million years he'd be having dinner and trading barbs with two Doms. How much his life has changed in just a few weeks. Coming to stay with Sean and Scott was just what he needed. Their kindness and fun-loving personalities were just the distraction he needed from the day's earlier nastiness. Not to mention his disappointment in having to delay his date with Wayne. Mikey would have to find a way to properly repay them for their generosity.

~

After dinner was served, it was clear Scott was wasting his talents as a short-order cook in a cafe. His cooking skills were that of a gourmet chef. His 'Beef Surprise' turned out to be perfectly cooked beef medallions with fresh garden vegetables and freshly made Bearnaise sauce. He even went as far as to make some quick homemade dinner rolls to accompany the meal. When Mikey took his first bite of the tender beef, he couldn't hold back a moan of pleasure. His hosts smiled wildly with amusement at his unguarded response, which in turn caused Mikey to blush.

Once dinner was over, the three men moved out to the large, covered entertainment deck at the back of the house. The open-air structure, which overlooked the river, featured a huge stone barbecue and outdoor dining table set, along with a large outdoor hot tub that looked big enough to fit a dozen people. The sun was just starting to set and the men were treated to an idyllic vista of a streaked evening sky, swirled with oranges and pinks, framed by the lilting branches of the gum trees that surrounded the house.

"Well," Scott said with his smooth baritone voice, "I think it's time we take a quick dip. I've been on my feet most of the day and I could use a soak."

With that, Scott and Sean began discarding the casual clothes they had quickly changed into shortly after arriving home. They were quickly down to their matching black swim shorts and climbing into the enormous hot tub, which Sean turned on. Mikey stood there, not quite sure what to do. When he'd packed his overnight bag, he hadn't thought to include swimwear.

"Are you going to join us, Mikey?" Sean asked kindly.

"Well, um, I didn't think to bring..."

"I left a pair of board shorts for you on the bed in the guest room. They might be a bit big on you, but you should be able to cinch them enough so they won't fall off."

"Oh! Thanks, Sean," Mikey said and he turned to go inside.

"But if they do fall off, boy," Scott said with a cheeky smile, "No one here will complain!" Sean splashed his partner and Scott scowled.

"Behave yourself," Sean admonished, chuckling, then turned to Mikey "Ignore him. If he keeps being naughty, I'll take him downstairs and give him a damn good thrashing."

"Not if I don't thrash you first..." Scott muttered under his breath.

Mikey laughed at his two new friends. They were unlike anybody he had ever met before, and he found their bizarre banter refreshing. He quickly went inside and changed into the board shorts.

When he returned, he slipped into the tub and was instantly surprised at just how warm the water was. Sean pressed a button that activated the bubbles and almost immediately, the water was moving and pulsing, gently vibrating every muscle in Mikey's body. It was like getting a full body massage underwater.

"I told you, boy," Scott said as he leaned back and relaxed, "This thing will undo every knot and ounce of stress in you. You'll be like jelly before you know it."

Scott wasn't wrong. Within minutes, Mikey's muscles slowly began to unwind and relax. He had no idea he had been carrying around this much tension until it finally began to melt away. He was soon warm, relaxed and content beyond words.

"I have *got* to get me one of these!" Mikey said, doing a terrible impression of Will Smith's character from the movie *Independence Day*. Sean and Scott laughed at his terrible joke.

After an hour in the hot tub, Mikey was relaxed but completely wiped out. He quickly towelled off, thanked his hosts for their kindness and retired to the guest room. As soon as he lay down on the gloriously soft pillow-top mattress, Mikey was drifting off to sleep, all thoughts of broken windows and prowlers, for the moment, forgotten.

Chapter Eight

AFTER SPENDING THE rest of the afternoon making enquiries around town, Wayne was no closer to identifying who was responsible for breaking Mikey's window. Everyone he spoke to was shocked to hear about such an incident occurring in their town. While he tried to downplay the homophobic angle to the attack, once he started asking people if they had heard anyone using homophobic language recently, it didn't take a rocket scientist to put two and two together.

Cooper's Landing, unlike a lot of country towns, was not the kind of place where homophobia was tolerated. A few years earlier, attitudes had been very different, and the town had learned a very valuable lesson about turning a blind eye to prejudice and bigotry.

These days, Gay people were not only accepted but welcomed with open arms. The Mayor had even once suggested the possibility of throwing an annual Pride parade. However, the idea was quickly abandoned when it was decided there simply weren't enough LGBTQ people living in Cooper's Landing to warrant an entire parade. Seeing a handful of people wandering awkwardly down the main street of town would not a parade make.

With no further leads to pursue, Wayne decided to call it a day. But before heading home, he made a point of passing by Mikey's house. Despite being early in the evening, Wayne noticed all the lights out and Mikey's ute missing. He briefly considered stopping and performing a welfare check, but figured that was an overreaction. Mikey had most likely just gone into town or was out for an evening drive. Wayne went home and, for the first time in a while, had an early night.

~

The next morning, Wayne was up bright and early and ready to take on a brand new day. After showering and dressing, he headed into town early so he can make a pit stop at the cafe for breakfast before work. He was surprised to see Mikey was already there, enjoying his usual coffee and croissant. Wayne quickly placed his order with Sean at the counter, then headed over to the city boy's table.

"Mind if I join you?"

"Not at all, have a seat," Mikey smiled and pulled out one of the chairs. Wayne sat down just as Scott, shaking his head and scowling, brought over a second cup of coffee for Mikey.

"Addict! I oughta beat it out of you..." Scott grumbled under his breath as he walked away.

"Any excuse to flog me, eh?" Mikey quipped, chuckling, which made Scott instantly smile and roll his eyes. Mikey took a sip of his drink, apparently unfussed by the bizarre exchange that he had just had with the intimidating Dom.

"Um, how are you feeling after everything yesterday?"

"Much better after last night. The Grinder Boys took me home with them and, wow! They sure know how to de-stress a man!"

Wayne nearly had a stroke. Mikey had spent the night with Sean *and* Scott? On the night they were supposed to be having a date?

"You... spent the night with them?"

"Oh, yeah," Mikey said absently, "Have you tried that hot tub of theirs? I swear that thing undid knots in muscles I didn't even know I had. I've never felt so loose and relaxed."

Wayne couldn't believe what he was hearing. Had he really blown his chances with Mikey this badly? Was Mikey the kind of guy who simply couldn't wait a few days for a date, so hopped into bed with whoever was available? Wayne had a hard time believing that.

"I'm sorry, I'm... just a little surprised. I had no idea you were into the whole..." Wayne made a cracking whip sound, and Mikey's eyes went wide before he burst out laughing.

"What? No! Not like that! We're just friends!"

Wayne was instantly flooded with relief.

"I didn't want to spend the night alone in the house since the locksmith couldn't make it out here until today, so the boys invited me to dinner at their place. It was a lovely evening, but I'm definitely not signing up for any recreational spankings," Mikey giggled and took another sip of his coffee.

Wayne suddenly felt very embarrassed. He should have made sure Mikey was comfortable staying at home after everything that had happened. He should have offered to take Mikey home with him.

"I'm so sorry, Mikey. If I had known you weren't feeling comfortable being alone, I would have come over or brought you around to my place for the night."

"That's sweet of you, but you have nothing to apologise for. If the locksmith had been able to come around yesterday, the whole thing would have been a non-issue. He's due out here this afternoon, so hopefully, everything will be back to normal by the end of the day."

Wayne was relieved that everything seemed to be okay between them. This bolstered his confidence, and he decided to take the initiative.

"Well, in that case, how about you and me have our date this evening? Assuming you don't have any other plans."

"No, no other plans. That sounds wonderful." Mikey beamed at him.

"Then it's a date. I'll pick you up at seven."

Mikey finished his coffee and made his goodbyes to the Grinder Boys and Wayne, then departed. While Wayne was sorry to see the cute city boy leave, he was feeling lighter than air, knowing that they would finally be having their first date that night.

"He's a good boy, that one," Sean said, appearing out of nowhere by Wayne's side, "It's about time you two pulled your socks up and went on a date."

"He sure is. We may have had a couple of misfires, but I've got a feeling tonight is going to be a memorable one." Wayne said, unable to hide his smile. Sean sat down and leaned in close.

"Mikey told us about everything that happened yesterday. Any ideas about who's responsible?"

"Not as yet. I've made some enquiries around town, but nobody seems to know anything. You guys haven't heard anything, have you? Any homophobic stuff or the like?"

"You'd be the first to know. I didn't think this kind of thing happened in Cooper's Landing anymore. Not after..."

"Yeah, I know. That's why I want to get this wrapped up ASAP. I want to squash it before this kind of behaviour starts to spread. We can't allow this sort of bigotry to fester in our town. Not again."

"If we hear anything, I promise to give you a shout. In the meantime, have a good time tonight. And don't do anything we wouldn't do!" Sean said with a wicked grin.

"I'm not sure what that would be. You guys seem to be pretty much open to anything!" Wayne said with a smirk.

Sean didn't comment further. He simply smiled like a Cheshire Cat and returned to his position behind the counter.

Wayne tucked into his breakfast and turned his thoughts to what he and Mikey could do on their date that night.

Chapter Nine

AFTER BREAKFAST, MIKEY headed over to the community hall at the other end of Main Street. The previous day had shown him that while he had two good friends in Sean and Scott, he didn't really know anyone else in town. Mikey wanted to rectify that by involving himself in more town activities, which should hopefully allow him to make more friends amongst the locals.

While doing some shopping at the general store a few days earlier, Mikey had noticed a community noticeboard near the cash registers. Amongst the multitude of paper notes pinned up on the board, advertising everything from babysitting services to the local Bachelors and Spinsters Ball, he had noticed a flyer about a local art competition and was keen to find out more. The flyer had directed him to contact 'Mavis' at the Country Women's Association. Since Mikey knew the community hall hosted CWA meetings, it was a good place to start looking for Mavis.

When he arrived, the car park was almost full and the whole area appeared to be a hive of activity, with ladies of all ages dashing in and out of the large hall, loading and unloading boxes from the parked cars.

The community hall was typical of most of the buildings in town, with its solid, red brick walls and corrugated iron roof. A large notice board by the front doors advertised a long list of current community events including Girl Guide and Boy Scout meetings, a town choir, a local amateur dramatics society and, of course, the regular meetings of the CWA.

Stepping inside, Mikey found dozens of women assembling and arranging tables and chairs into long rows, almost like a production line, while others began unpacking boxes filled with what appeared to be kitchen utensils.

"Who are you looking for, my love?" A kindly, mature woman with a cat-themed cardigan said.

"I was looking for Mavis. Is she here?"

"MAVIS!!!" the woman called out loudly, "She'll be out in a minute, pet."

A few moments later, an older woman, dressed primly with her silver hair in a bun, emerged from a large crowd at the back of the hall. Cardigan Lady pointed her to Mikey, and the woman smiled and immediately approached him.

"You must be Mikey! How lovely to finally meet you. Welcome to Cooper's Landing!" she said, enveloping Mikey in a warm, but thoroughly unexpected hug.

"Um, thank you very much. I wanted to ask about the art competition."

"Oh, yes. I'd heard around town that you were a painter. Interested in entering?" Mikey nodded, still a little dazed from the hug.

"Well, you're just in time. Entries close at five pm today. The entry fee is $10 per artwork submitted. It's all for a good cause – Meals on Wheels – and the first prize is $100. Winners are announced at the Annual Town Fair next Saturday."

"Town Fair? I haven't heard about that."

"Over at the public park. Kicks off at ten am. All the usual stuff. Food stalls, rides, games, flea market, art competition, lamington drive..."

"Lamington drive? I haven't had a lamington since I was a kid!"

Mavis smiled kindly, "That's what we're doing here today. We're setting up to assemble and pack up all the lamingtons into boxes, ready for sale on Saturday. We should make a fortune for our local charities this year."

"Well, I don't have anything planned until this afternoon. Do you need some help?" Mikey asked, keen to involve himself, especially if there were lamingtons on offer. He could still remember helping to make the chocolate and coconut-coated sponge cakes with his childhood nanny. At least until his father had put an end to it.

Apparently, his son was 'above mucking about in the kitchen with the help.'

"We can always use an extra pair of hands. Plus we need someone to help transport the packed lamingtons to the General Store. We're keeping them in their walk-in fridge until Saturday."

"I'm all yours then. Lead the way!" Mikey said with a smile, and Mavis looked at him like he walked on water. While he did find her overly friendly, especially with that hug and the way she was currently walking him around the hall on her arm, but he suspected this must be how she buttered up the volunteers. Mikey didn't mind, it was all for a good cause after all.

~

They spent most of the morning making lamingtons on the production line, followed by packing them up into boxes of six and tying them up with pretty blue ribbons. Once packaged, the boxes were packed into large cardboard cartons and sent off in loads to the general store. Mavis and Mikey were on their fourth run to the store, and their conversation had been free and easy.

"So," Mavis asked absently as she watched the scenery of the town whizz by, "Have any handsome young men taken your fancy since you've been in town?"

"And what makes you quite so sure that I'm gay, Mavis?" Mikey said with a smirk.

"Oh, please, honey! The whole town knows you're gay. Nobody cares!"

"Somebody cares, as my front window will attest too." Mikey thought to himself.

"Well, there is one guy. We're having our first date tonight, actually."

"Really? Tell me all about him. Is he a local? Does he have a nice bum?"

"Mavis! You're a wild woman!" Mikey hooted with laughter.

"You better believe it – now dish!"

"Okay, okay. He's the local cop. Really friendly. Helped me out on my first day in town and I haven't been able to stop thinking about him since."

"Oh, Wayne?" Mavis said, sounding oddly excited, "He's a lovely young man. Always sweet to his mother. I reckon you two will be like two peas in a pod. So where are you going on your date?"

"We'll probably head out to the diner. There aren't a lot of dining options in town from what I'm told. But I don't mind. I just want to get to know him better."

"That's so lovely. Well, good luck to you, my dear. Hopefully, it'll be a night to remember."

~

It was mid-afternoon by the time Mikey dropped Mavis back at the community centre. The locksmith was due to arrive at his house shortly, so he would need to be making tracks. He had made a brief detour to the ranch earlier to pick up one of his paintings to give to Mavis for the art competition. She had been very enthusiastic, and Mikey hoped the judges liked his work as much as she did. He helped Mavis put the painting in the back of her car before bidding her farewell.

"Good luck with the date tonight, sweetheart!" Mavis called out as she drove away in her little hatchback, leaving Mikey alone in the now virtually deserted car park. He was about to get into his car when he noticed what looked like a man hiding in the bushes at the other end of the parking lot. When their eyes met, the man dashed away into the scrub. Mikey gave chase, calling out to him, but within moments he was gone.

He had only seen him for a moment, but the man had appeared to be vaguely familiar. Mikey couldn't quite put his finger on from where. Strange. But he didn't have time to think about it. He needed to get out to the ranch and meet the locksmith. He also needed to start getting ready for his date with Wayne. He returned to the car and drove away, unaware that he was still being observed from the bushes.

Chapter Ten

WAYNE HAD BARELY finished his breakfast at Grinder Boys when he received a call out to the pub down the road after someone contacted the station reporting two intoxicated persons causing property damage. He jumped in his car and headed down Main Street toward the Royal Hotel.

When he arrived, Wayne found the bar section of the pub was closed, not due to open until eleven AM, but could hear a commotion coming from inside. Running around the side of the building to the hotel's reception office, he found two young men, in their early twenties, smashing the place up while the hotel manager cowered defencelessly behind the reception desk. Wayne drew his taser and pointed it towards the bigger of the two men.

"Police! Hands where I can see them – now!"

The two men froze in place, their eyes wide with shock. Wayne could see instantly that the men were not drunk, but very much under the influence of something. In all his time as a police officer in Cooper's Landing, he had never once had to deal with a drug-related crime. Alcohol, yes. But never drugs.

The smaller man attempted to rush Wayne, but he was able to subdue him with the taser, falling to the ground screaming as the electricity passed through him. His larger friend dropped to his knees with his hands in the air, the man looking visibly confused, and promptly burst into tears.

Once he had both men handcuffed and secured in the back of his vehicle, he verified that the hotel manager was uninjured. She reported that the two men were out-of-towners passing through. They had apparently checked in the previous evening. The manager went on to describe having received several noise complaints from other guests during the night, as the men were loudly partying in their room. When the two men had come downstairs that morning, wanting to stay another day, the manager had refused. That's when they started tearing the place apart. A quick search of the men's hotel room found a small quantity of what appeared to be meth, which explained the erratic and violent behaviour.

Since he didn't have the facilities to hold two prisoners, and these men needed to be checked over by paramedics, Wayne called ahead to Bushman's Pass Police and informed them of his intent to transfer two prisoners into their charge.

"So much for a quiet day," Wayne grumbled to himself. Driving all the way to Bushman's Pass with two meth heads, then driving all the way back home was not how he had intended to spend his day.

Wayne wasn't happy about drugs in his town. He needed to know if this was an isolated incident, or something more dangerous. The two men didn't feel very chatty on their long drive to Bushman's Pass, so Wayne was left with a lot of unanswered questions. Who were these guys? Where did they get the drugs? Were the drugs bought locally or did they bring them from home? Hopefully, the boys at Bushman's Pass station would get him some answers.

~

By the time Wayne got back to Cooper's Landing, it was almost three PM. Shirl was busy filing paperwork and organising documents for Wayne to sign. He sat down at his desk and started writing out his report on the hotel incident so he could send it through to Bushman's Pass as soon as possible. Before he realised, it was past five PM and Shirl had left for the day.

He quickly wrapped up his paperwork and closed up the station for the night. It may have been a long day filled with frustration, but one thing had helped get Wayne through it – the thought of his first date with a certain cute city boy that night. He quickly drove home to shower and change. He didn't have long until he was due at Mikey's place.

Pulling up at the Riverside Ranch just before seven, Wayne couldn't help but feel nervous. This was his first proper date in a long time. Not a blind date or some horrible fix-up to appease his mother, but an actual date with a guy he was really interested in. Things had to go right tonight. He'd wished he could have organised something a little classier than dinner at the town diner, but restaurant choices were few and far between in a small town like Cooper's Landing. He could have, maybe, thrown together a home-cooked meal at home, but he would have needed more time to prepare for that – plus Wayne wasn't confident his grilled chops with three veg would be any more impressive than anything the diner could provide.

When he knocked on the door, he quickly straightened his shirt, smoothed his hair back and checked his breath by huffing into his palm. The fact that he had done all these things at least a dozen times since he had left his house was neither here nor there. It had become a nervous tick by now. The door opened and Wayne's mouth went dry.

Mikey was standing in the doorway, looking more amazing than ever. He wore a pair of tight black jeans that showed off his legs and round arse; a dark blue button-up and black casual boots. Mikey's hair was immaculate and he was freshly shaven. Wayne was coincidently wearing a similar outfit, but somehow Mikey made it look like something off a fashion parade.

"Hi, you're right on time! You scrub up good, Sarge," Mikey said with a wicked grin.

"Thanks, you too. Are you ready to go?"

"Absolutely. You lead the way."

Wayne did just that, taking Mikey's hand in his and escorting him to his patrol car. Once buckled in, Wayne started the engine and proceeded down the driveway and out onto the road.

"So, the diner?" Mikey said, breaking the silence, "I haven't had a chance to try it out yet. Is it good?"

"It's probably not as fancy as the places you're used to in the big city, but it's a great place for a feed," Wayne confessed. He was still a little ashamed he hadn't planned something more elaborate for their first date.

"Wayne, I'm not nearly as fancy as you seem to think I am. I promise. If they do a decent burger, I guarantee I'll be in heaven."

"Then you're in luck," Wayne smiled, "Order the Works burger with 'the lot' and you'll be in for a treat."

Mikey smiled wide and said he looked forward to trying it. Wayne relaxed knowing Mikey would be happy eating at the diner. He'd been worried Mikey would be expecting them to serve sushi or some fancy French cuisine like a Melbourne restaurant. Finding out Mikey was a lot more down to earth than Wayne had initially given him credit for had taken a lot of the pressure off what would hopefully be a nice, casual evening. Plus he knew for a fact that the diner served some pretty epic hamburgers. Their 'works' burger was something of a local legend. Famous for its size and its insane amount of fillings, Mikey would love it.

When they pulled up at the diner, Wayne jumped out of the car first to get Mikey's door. He then held the door for Mikey when they entered the diner. Wayne realised he was probably going a bit overboard, but being a gentleman was something his mother had ingrained into him from an early age. Besides, he liked the idea of doing these things for his handsome date.

The hostess escorted them to a quiet booth at the back of the restaurant that had clearly been reserved for them. Somehow, news of their date has spread. Mikey looked at their table then looked at Wayne, his expression a combination of amusement and puzzlement. Unlike the other tables in the greasy spoon-style establishment, their table was adorned with a crisp white tablecloth, cloth napkins, a single red rose in a silver vase and even a lit candle. Wayne nodded to the hostess, subtly indicating his happiness with the table. The hostess smiled as they sat down, pleased that her hard work was appreciated. She issued them with menus and took their drink orders, then disappeared out the back.

"Did you organise all this? You shouldn't have gone to so much trouble!" Mikey said in a hushed tone.

"I wish I could take credit for it, but I didn't even make a reservation. They don't *do* reservations here. Looks like news of our date has spread all over town."

"Oh, that might be my fault. I spent the day down at the community centre, making lamingtons with the CWA. I made a new friend while I was there, and I mentioned in passing that I was going on a date tonight."

It was while Mikey was talking about his new friend from the community centre, his spidey-sense started tingling. He looked across the diner and saw a woman sitting on one of the bar stools. She was wearing a silk scarf over her hair and large sunglasses, while she rather unsubtly hid behind one of the diner's large laminated menus. He didn't need to be Sherlock Holmes to uncover who this mystery woman was. His mother was not exactly a master of disguise.

Wayne was not impressed. This went beyond her normal gossiping. This was straight-up stalking. "Not cool, Mum. Not cool." he thought to himself.

"This... friend... of yours," Wayne asked, "She wouldn't be an older lady by the name of Mavis, would she?"

"Yes! Have you met her?"

"Oh, I know her, alright..." Wayne muttered to himself.

"Well, I met her because she's running the annual charity art show this weekend..."

"Charity Art Show? What the hell was she up to?" Wayne thought.

He asked Mikey to tell him everything, and he describes how Mavis had told him about raising money for Meals on Wheels, how he paid her an entry fee and, most disturbingly of all, about some cash prize for the winner.

"Why? Is something wrong?" Mikey said, looking a little confused as to why he was being interrogated about this.

"I'm sorry, but I have to make a confession. There is no annual art show. I've lived here my entire life, and there has never been one to my knowledge."

"You mean, Mavis is a scam artist?" Mikey was shocked.

"Yes, but not the kind you're thinking of. Oh, God! This is so embarrassing!" Wayne could feel his cheeks reddening. He would kill his mother for this.

"What is?" Mikey reached over the table and put his hand over Wayne's.

"Mavis is my Mum. She's the local gossip queen. I suspect she was trying to meet you so she could get the inside goss on you." Wayne took a fortifying breath, then continued, "I'd told her that I liked you, and before I knew what was happening, she and her friends were out trying to learn everything they could about you."

"So that's why everyone was asking me if I were gay within about 5 seconds of meeting me!" Mikey said, trying not to laugh.

"Oh god, they didn't?" Wayne groaned and put his head in his hands.

"Don't worry about it." Mikey chuckled, "There's no harm done. My Aunt Geri sounds very similar to your Mum. Always needs to be on top of the latest gossip."

"Except, your Aunt Geri isn't in disguise and hiding on the other side of the diner right now!" Wayne whispered.

Mikey's eyes went as wide as saucers before he burst out laughing. Wayne did not expect this reaction. He thought Mikey would storm out and never want to speak to him again.

"Well, your Mum sounds like she really cares about you, if she's willing to go to these lengths to make sure your date goes off without a hitch."

"Yeah, but I can't let this go unchallenged. Gossip is one thing. But she's technically committed crimes now. Obtaining money by deception. Falsely representing a charity. She can't do stuff like that."

"Oh, I entirely agree. She must be punished. So, what are we going to do about it?"

"*We?*" Wayne thought to himself, confused.

"Well, um, I'll have a word with her about it."

"Something tells me you've 'had a word with her' about stuff like this in the past?" Mikey said, his expression sly.

"Yeah."

"Doesn't seem to have worked all that well. Perhaps..." Mikey said, pondering something for a moment, "Perhaps we should try a different approach this time? Perhaps we should see what happens when the tables are turned?" Mikey said with a smirk that Wayne could only describe as diabolical.

~

Once Mikey's had explained his complete plan, Wayne was stunned into silence. The cute city boy was not nearly as innocent he had initially thought he was. Mikey was, in fact, an evil genius. His plan could work, but could Wayne really go through with it? He had tried reasoning with his mother in the past, but she always ended up falling back on her gossipy, interfering ways. Perhaps Mikey was right, and a new approach may be warranted? After careful consideration, Wayne agreed to the plan and they set about finishing their meals. They would implement their devious little plot immediately.

As they stood and headed toward the exit, Wayne saw that his mother was still at the counter, feebly attempting to hide behind her menu. That's when Mikey struck.

"Mavis? Is that you?" Mikey cried out, smiling and embracing Wayne's shocked mother, "It's so lovely to see you again!"

"Oh, hello dear," Mavis said, clearly not expecting to be spotted, "What a coincidence seeing you here."

Wayne stood there silently, aiming a scowl at his mother, and he could read in her eyes that she knew she was busted.

"Let me introduce you to my date, Mavis. He's the one I was telling you about! Mavis, this is Wayne. Wayne this is Mavis!" Mikey enthused with a giant grin on his face. He was playing this role perfectly, but Wayne focused on keeping his face neutral.

"Yes, we've met," Wayne said gruffly, narrowing his eyes at a now pale Mavis.

"Of course, you know each other. Small towns and all that..."

"Um, well actually..." Mavis tried to interrupt, but Mikey was on a roll.

"That's the great thing about these little country towns. That's why I moved here. Everyone knows everyone. Everyone looks out for each other. And above all else, people are kind, caring and honest with each other. None of that backstabbing and underhandedness that I always had to put up with back in the city."

"Mikey," Wayne cut him off before he laid it on too thick, "I'm afraid I have to tell you something." as Mavis watched on in horror, her lips quivering and eyes wide.

"What is it, Wayne? Is something wrong?" Mikey said dramatically, instantly looking crestfallen. If Wayne didn't know he was acting, his saddened expression would have broken his heart.

"I lied to you!" Mavis suddenly interjected, her outburst silencing the entire diner. All eyes were on our little group. Wayne noticed that several of the more senior gossipers in town were giving them their rapt attention, "I'm Wayne's mother. I'm sorry, I didn't mean any harm, I swear it. I just wanted to get to know you, so you and Wayne could get together. He said he liked you and I was afraid if he waited too long, you might slip through his fingers!"

"Oh, Mavis! How could you!" Mikey exclaimed, his performance getting a little overdramatic, "I'll never be able to trust again!"

"Alright, Lawrence Olivier! That's enough. I don't want her to get a guilt overdose."

"Awww!" Mikey said, immediately breaking off his performance, "I was really getting into my character. I was about to cry and everything!"

"Maybe next time." Wayne chuckled, shaking his head.

"Um, what the hell is going on?" Mavis said, looking suitably perplexed.

"Never mind about that, Mum. How about you explain to me about this so-called charity art show?" Wayne said, adopting his official cop voice. Mavis was momentarily struck speechless by the conversational whiplash.

"I... I... I was just trying to get you two to meet each other. Mrs Abernathy told me that Mikey was interested in art, so I thought an art competition would be a good way of getting you both at the same place at the same time..."

"And you charged him some sort of entry fee?" Wayne encouraged.

"It was for a good cause. Every penny goes to the Meals of Wheels." Mavis said as if she had just scored a major point.

"Mum! You know as well as I do, there is no Meals on Wheels service in Cooper's Landing."

Mavis visibly crumpled, she clearly had not expected Wayne to know that.

"Are you serious?" Mikey chimed in, clearly outraged at this revelation. Wayne was now wondering if this was part of the plan or if he was genuinely shocked. Wayne was going to have his hands full with this one.

"Do you realise how serious this is, Mum? The position you've put me in? I have no choice, you realise that, right?"

"Choice in what?" Mavis said, now looking absolutely baffled.

"Time to kick Mikey's plan into high gear." Wayne thought, as he straightened his shoulders and cleared his throat. He reached into his back pocket and pulled out the handcuffs he carried at all times, even when off-duty. He quickly opened them with a practiced hand and held them up. He stepped forward and loomed over his mother.

"Mum... Mavis Townsend, you're under arrest."

"What?!" his Mum squawked, "You're joking, right?"

"You do not have to say anything, but anything you do say will be recorded and used against you in a court of law..."

As he turned his stunned mother around and began handcuffing her, he continued reciting her rights, all while the entire diner gasped and started whispering amongst themselves. Wayne noticed a few people pulling out their phones, clearly taking pictures and texting their friends.

"You can't do this! What are the charges?" Mavis said, suddenly realising this was not a joke.

"Misappropriation of funds. Misrepresentation of a charity. Operating a cash prize competition without a license. Need I go on?"

"But it wasn't like that! I swear!"

"Do you always bring handcuffs on a first date?" Mikey asked quietly, his lips curled in a slight smirk.

"Well, you never know..." Wayne replied as he finished cuffing his mother and began escorting her out to his car, Mikey following in their wake.

"What? You thought you would get to handcuff me for kinky bondage fun after just one date?" Mikey said, sounding scandalised.

"No! I meant, I'm the only cop in town, so I always carry cuffs with me. You never know when I'm going to need them." to which Mikey laughed at his obvious mistake.

"Just out of interest, though," Wayne asked as he opened the back door of his 4WD and guided his still-protesting mother into the seat,

"How many dates does it take to get to the kinky bondage fun?" he said with a wicked gleam in his eyes.

"I think you're drunk with power, Sargent. Now hurry up and throw your mother in the slammer."

~

Wayne hadn't been sure how this first date with Mikey was going to go, but he had never imagined it would end with him handcuffing his mother and placing her under arrest.

"This is the best first date ever!" Wayne exclaimed, his smile wide, as he drove down the dark street toward the police station.

"I'm so glad I could provide you with such awesome entertainment," Mavis grumbled from the backseat, "You know I'm going to kill you for this!"

"Threatening the life of a police officer? What's that worth?" Mikey asked.

"That's twenty to life!" Wayne crowed, not even attempting to hide his mirth now.

"Damn it, Wayne! This isn't funny anymore! Let me go this instant!"

"I'm afraid it's out of my hands now, Mum. The only person who can drop the charges is Mikey here. And he seems very keen on seeing justice served." Wayne chuckled.

"I didn't mean any harm. Please! Please don't do this Mikey!" Mavis wailed as they pulled up outside the police station.

"Alright, Alright. I'll drop the charges on one condition."

Mikey never mentioned this part when he went over the plan. Wayne wondered what he was up to.

"Name it!" Mavis said desperately.

"A cup of tea," Mikey said simply.

"Huh?" Wayne and Mavis said together.

"Let's go back to your place. We can all sit down and you can make us a cup of tea. You know, the normal way someone gets to know someone? Oh, and I want my ten bucks back."

"Oh, he was good. He was really good." Wayne thought. Bravo, Mikey!

"Done!" Mavis agreed readily.

"Can't I at least throw her in the cells first?" Wayne begged, really keen to get a picture of his Mum behind bars. Mikey gave him an incredulous look. Wayne wondered briefly if he *was* drunk with power.

Wayne sighed, pulled away from the police station and drove toward his mother's house. When they arrived, Wayne quickly released Mavis from the very loosely fitted handcuffs before she disappeared inside to put the kettle on.

When Wayne and Mikey stepped inside, Mavis handed over the ill-gotten ten dollars and tried to return the painting he had entered in the non-existent art competition.

"Actually, Mavis, I'd like you to keep it."

"Really? Are you sure?"

"Of course. Hang it up somewhere in your home. That way, every time you look at it, it can serve as a reminder of your dastardly crime spree." Mikey said with a smirk.

Mavis blushed and set about making the tea. Wayne just shook his head, chuckling. This city boy was pure evil – and he loved it.

Chapter Eleven

AFTER SEVERAL CUPS of tea and slices of Mavis' homemade cinnamon cake, Mikey and Wayne decide to leave the criminal mastermind to her own devices. Mikey thought it was so sweet how Wayne and his mother had such a close, loving relationship – something Mikey had never got to have with his own mother. He watched on as the tall, hulking policeman bent down to kiss his small but diminutive mother on the cheek before bidding her farewell.

"The night's still young," Wayne said as they approached the 4WD, "If you're not in a hurry to go home, there's something I'd like to show you."

"I think I have an opening in my schedule," Mikey said with a cheeky grin as Wayne, ever the gentlemen, held the passenger-side door open for his date.

"Great, I want to show you the best view in town."

Wayne drove them through town then out past the river bend at the end of Main Street, toward the tall hills on the outskirts of town. They followed along a dirt track, the road in total darkness except for the 4WD's headlights. They eventually reached a small parking area next to a gap in the treeline. Another vehicle was parked there, but upon seeing the police car parking next to it, it promptly started its engine and drove away.

"Let me guess," Mikey said with a smirk, "The local Lover's Lane?"

"How did you guess?"

"The looks on those two teenager's faces when you pulled up next to them. I've never seen such a look of panic!" he chuckled.

"Well, you're right. But I promise I'm not trying to push for anything. I really did just want to show you the view. Come on, you're gonna love this." said Wayne as he jumped out of the vehicle and bounded around to open Mikey's door.

"Close your eyes. Keep them closed until I tell you to open them."

"Seriously?" Mikey said, "It's a bit dark for..."

"I'll guide you. Do you trust me?"

"Yes," Mikey said without hesitation, noticing that this answer seemed to please his date inordinately. He closed his eyes and took hold of Wayne's hand. He allowed himself to be guided across what felt like a dirt track, then a small patch of grass before stopping.

"Keep 'em closed," Wayne muttered from behind Mikey, as he carefully adjusted Mikey's position by guiding him by the shoulders. Mikey was curious as to what this was all about.

"Okay, open your eyes and look straight ahead."

Mikey carefully did as instructed, and he couldn't believe what he was seeing. Before him was a stunning twilight vista of twinkling lights. The town below in the valley was like a string of dull fairy lights, and the clear sky above was a carpet of shining stars that almost reflected the lights below. Looking straight ahead, the whole visage gave the effect of being surrounded by stars.

"Wow! This is gorgeous! It's almost like I'm standing in space with stars all around me."

"I told you you'd like it. This spot is my favourite place in the world. So quiet, so peaceful. I've never shared it with anyone before, but I knew I had to share it with you."

"Thank you," Mikey turned to face Wayne, "This is amazing. Growing up in the city, I never really appreciated stuff like this. Then I came here, and it's like seeing the sky for the first time."

"I used to come here all the time. If I ever needed to get away from everything or I just wanted to be by myself, I'd come here. Not at night usually, I guess that would be weird with all the teenagers necking. But even during the day, the view is spectacular. We'll have to come back here so I can show you. You won't believe how different it looks by the light of day."

"I'd like that," Mikey said, turning back to look at the stars. Wayne moved up behind him and gently wrapped his arms around Mikey, hooking his chin on Mikey's shoulder. Mikey leaned into the embrace and the two men watched the splendorous view in silence.

~

"So, what is it that you actually do for a living? When I asked you before, you were a little cryptic," Wayne said later as they slowly walked back along the dirt track toward the car, "You wouldn't believe the rumours going around town about you."

"Oh let me guess, international jewel thief? Spy? Human trafficker?"

"Why would you assume everyone in town thinks you're some kind of criminal?"

"I dunno. The way this town gossips, nothing would surprise me."

"Well, you wouldn't believe the current theory doing the rounds."

"Oh, God, dare I ask?"

"They think you're Banksy."

Mikey looked at him blankly, trying to process that information.

"That's what they think? How the hell did they come to that conclusion?"

"A mysterious city guy moves to town. Asks about art supplies at the General Store. Lives alone on an isolated property..."

"That's insane!"

"That's Cooper's Landing," Wayne shrugged, "It gets worse."

"How?"

"Someone spilt a bucket of paint outside the hardware store the other day. It sent the rumours into overdrive, and now the Mayor wants to preserve it as a historical landmark. There's even talk of a dedication ceremony."

"I'm sorry to disappoint you and the whole of Cooper's Landing, but I'm not Banksy," Mikey said with a sly smirk.

"Isn't that exactly what Banksy would say?" Wayne chuckled.

"I wouldn't know. I'm not Banksy!" Mikey laughed.

"Well, if you aren't Banksy, what the hell are you?"

"Honestly? I guess, technically, I'm unemployed."

"If you're unemployed, how can you afford to buy a ranch, a new car..?"

"I guess I'm what you would call 'independently wealthy' so I don't really need a job. I used to be a financial trader in the city. A pretty successful one too. But it wasn't making me happy, following the path my father was laying out for me. Sure, making myself and my clients rich was great, but what was the point if I never had a moment to enjoy any of it? I wanted to do something else with my life. I wanted a quieter pace of life. I wanted to explore my art. So I quit my job, much to my father's fury, packed up my life and moved out here."

Wayne looked at him like this was the most insane choice anyone could ever have made, and in many ways, he was probably right. But Mikey knew that despite the risks of moving his entire life out into the middle of nowhere, it was the best decision he had ever made.

"So what about you? Tell me about becoming a cop."

"Not much to tell. I saw the recruitment posters, seeking LGBT recruits to serve as liaison officers. When I asked about it, the old Sarge encouraged me to apply. I went to the academy, did my station-based training in Albury, then transferred back to Cooper's Landing."

"No regrets coming back here?" Mikey asked as they reached the car.

"Not for a second. Besides, better than being a big-city cop. All those drugs and guns? Luckily we don't have much of that stuff out this way. Although the boys from Bushman's Pass have been getting more and more drug problems pop up in their neck of the woods recently. Nah, I'm happy right here. Best place of Earth."

"It sure is," Mikey said breathlessly, looking into Wayne's eyes. Wayne gently moved forward, tilted his head down and brought their lips together in a sweet, tender kiss. Heat flooded through Mikey as he opened his mouth slightly, subtly signalling for Wayne to deepen the kiss. A spark of electricity passed between them as their tongues tentatively met.

It was then Wayne's phone started ringing, breaking the moment. Wayne let out a frustrated groan.

"I'm so sorry. Duty calls." Wayne said, reluctantly stepping back.

"It's okay, I get it. Take the call."

"Cooper's Landing Police..." Wayne said, answering his phone, as Mikey set to step away to give him some privacy. But Wayne grabbed a hold of Mikey by the arm, halting his departure.

"No, we'll be there in ten minutes, Robbo. Thanks for the head's up." Wayne said, ending the call, "Get in the car, we have to go now."

"What's happening?"

"That was Robbo, the captain of the local rural fire service. He says there's a building on fire out near the highway. It's your ranch."

Mikey's blood ran cold.

Chapter Twelve

THE RAGING INFERNO was throwing thick plumes of smoke into the inky black sky. Tiny, orange embers danced above the licking flames like fireflies as the firefighters desperately attempted to bring the massive wall of flames under control. Even from the road, as Wayne and Mikey approached the ranch, it was clear the structure was completely engulfed by the fire.

Wayne pulled the 4WD into the driveway and parked a safe distance from both the burning building and the fire trucks that were attempting to contain the blaze. Mikey gasped as he took in the chaotic scene that surrounded them.

"Thankfully, it's just the barn," Wayne tried to reassure Mikey, "And hopefully the boys can stop it from spreading to the rest of the buildings."

Mikey nodded silently, clearly in shock. His eyes were wide as he watched the old barn. Now just a shell consumed by angry flames, the roof began to sag and collapse in on itself. The building was a write-off. No chance of saving it. All the firefighters could do now was stop the fire from spreading. The last thing the area needed was an uncontrolled bushfire.

"How could this have happened?" Mikey asked breathlessly.

"I don't know. But we'll find out. Stay here while I get an update on what's happening. I'll be back shortly," Wayne said.

"Okay. Thanks." Mikey said absently, transfixed by the flames.

Wayne was instantly in official mode as he left the vehicle and approached the fire scene, looking for Robbo, the fire captain. He had a sinking feeling that this fire was no accident. It didn't take long to find his old friend.

Robbo was a tall, bulky man with a large, bushy black beard. His face was wet with sweat and smeared with soot, matching the bright yellow jumpsuit uniform he wore. Wayne had known the man since they were both boys playing footy together back in high school. So when he saw the grim expression on the fire fighter's face, it said it all.

"Please tell me this was an accident. Faulty wiring or something?" Wayne asked, knowing full well the old barn wasn't wired up for electricity.

"Sorry, mate. Definitely arson. The whole barn was doused inside and out with accelerant, probably petrol. We've already found several jerry cans scattered around, all badly burned. Not sure if they're related or not, since the barn was filled with tonnes of old junk."

"Damn it," Wayne said through gritted teeth, "I'll establish a crime scene. Once the fire is out, I'll gather up whatever evidence I can. See what the forensics team in Bushman's Pass can determine."

"The barn has almost burned itself out. We should have the area secured within the next hour or so. But it'll be morning before it'll be cool enough for you to go in."

The two men walked over to the 4WD, Wayne introduced Robbo to Mikey and together they broke the news. Mikey quickly launched himself out of the vehicle, needing air. Wayne could see the younger man was desperately trying not to freak out, but it was clear he was getting to his stress limit. Robbo excused himself, needing to return to his crew.

"Who the hell could be doing this?" Mikey said sharply, "What have I done to deserve this?"

"Nothing. This isn't your fault. This is the work of a sick and dangerous mind. It was pure luck that the fireys got here in time. You would have lost the whole ranch, not to mention the surrounding countryside would have gone up in flames with it. It doesn't take much for a small fire to turn into a full-blown bushfire. Whoever did this clearly didn't care they were endangering hundreds of lives with this stupid and dangerous stunt."

"Oh my God! I didn't even realise it's bushfire season. Is the town going to be safe?" Mikey asked, looking stricken.

"Robbo and the boys have the fire contained. He reckons they'll have it out soon. But if they'd been just a few minutes later..." Wayne left the grim thought unspoken, "When I find whoever did this, they're going to get hit with some serious charges."

Wayne escorted Mikey inside the main ranch house so he could rest, but it was immediately clear that he wouldn't be able to stay there that night. The whole house stank of smoke.

"Go and pack an overnight bag. You can stay at my place tonight."

Mikey looked at him with a raised eyebrow.

"I have a guest room," Wayne assured him, "You know, so you won't be able to take advantage of me."

"Dork," Mikey smirked.

"That's Sergeant Dork to you," Wayne said, making Mikey laugh softly. Wayne was glad that amidst all this chaos, he was at least able to distract Mikey briefly with a joke. Even if it did mean making fun of himself.

"Not quite the way I expected our first date to end," Mikey said as he started stuffing some clothes into a backpack.

"Me either. Although, on the upside, I did get to arrest my mother. So it's not all bad."

Mikey smirked, "Do you think she'll ever forgive you for that?"

"It'll be a cold day in hell before she makes her special pavlova again, but I suspect the fact that we actually went on a date together is keeping her happy."

Once Mikey had finished packing, Wayne escorted him back out to the 4WD. Wayne knew he would have to return to the ranch once the fire crews had finished. He would need to secure the scene, then start the arduous task of combing through the burnt rubble for evidence. Wayne was not looking forward to that.

~

Wayne's house was nothing special, just a little two-bedroom cottage a few streets from the police station. The front yard was just grass with no flower beds. Wayne didn't have time to plant and maintain a proper garden like his Mum's place. He barely had time to run a mower over the lawn most weekends. But he was proud of his house. He kept it neat and tidy, inside and out, and while some people, mainly his mother, had complained the interior lacked personality, Wayne was the first to admit that he wasn't an interior decorator and was rarely home for anything more than crashing out after a long day at work.

"Wow, it's pretty," Mikey said when they pulled into the driveway. Wayne wasn't sure if he was being entirely sincere, considering Mikey lived in a recently renovated ranch house, and Wayne's place certainly didn't compare. Wayne was already apprehensive about having Mikey over, despite quickly extending an invitation when it became clear that his house would not be habitable until properly aired out. Mikey, who was used to his big city life and even bigger bank account, was sure to notice that Wayne's little house was a big step down from what he was accustomed to. Despite being attracted to each other and having gotten on well so far, a niggling voice in the back of his head kept whispering to him that Wayne simply wasn't good enough. That Mikey would eventually realise that dating a small-town cop was a dead end.

"Is everything okay?" Mikey said, breaking him out of his thoughts.

"Sure. Let's get you inside. I imagine you must be exhausted."

"A shower and a good night's sleep wouldn't go astray, I can tell you that."

The two men went inside, stepping into the living room. It was sparsely decorated, much like the rest of the house, but the big old sofa was comfy and the TV was huge – perfect for watching the football on the odd occasion Wayne was able to catch a game.

"Oh, look at that screen!" Mikey said with excitement, "We are so having a Movie Night sometime. It's like a cinema screen!"

Wayne felt himself blush. He always suspected his TV was too big, but he didn't splash out on fancy stuff often. He loved falling asleep on the couch in front of the box, especially with a favourite movie playing. Doing that cuddled up with a certain cute city boy didn't sound bad at all.

"Sounds like fun. We'll have to set it up sometime," Wayne smiled, "Come on through to the guest room and we'll get you set up."

They wandered down the hall to the guest bedroom, situated opposite the bathroom. The room wasn't huge but it was comfortable. Mikey put his overnight bag down and sat on the bed, giving the mattress a little test bounce.

"The sheets are clean and fresh. I just changed them the other day. The bathroom is across the hall, so help yourself to the shower. I'm going to head off to the station."

"Calling in the forensics team?" Mikey asked.

"Actually, I *am* the forensics team. I'll secure the scene, gather any evidence I can find and send it off to Bushman's Pass for analysis."

"Jeez, you have to be a jack of all trades to be a country cop, don't you?" Mikey said, looking concerned.

"Pretty much. It's not easy, but I do what I can to keep my town safe. I live in hope that one day they'll increase my budget so I can get another officer or two someday. But for now, it's down to me to get the job done."

"Well, you have my full confidence. I'm just worried that you're working too hard. Surely your superiors must realise that all of this is far too much for one man." Mikey said, getting up from the bed and taking Wayne's hand in his and giving it a gentle squeeze.

"It's government bean-counters that determine the budget, unfortunately. They would have shut the station down years ago if they could. But legally a town this size has to have a permanent police presence *if* the nearest police station is more than 150km away. Doesn't stop them reducing the budget, though."

"That's terrible."

"Worse still, they might end up closing us down anyway. The town's population is shrinking. Between older residents dying and younger people moving out to the city rather than staying here, we're not far from losing the minimum population requirements. Cooper's Landing has already lost the bank and the post office. Many people feel if the police station goes too, then it's the beginning of the end of the town."

Mikey enveloped him in a warm hug, pressing his long, lithe body against his. Wayne returned the hug, smoothing his hands down the city boy's back.

"I had no idea the situation was so bad here. Surely there's something that can be done?"

"Why do you think everyone was so super friendly when you first moved here? New residents are a sign that the town's misfortunes are turning around."

Mikey made no attempt to break the hug. He just lay his head down on Wayne's chest and closed his eyes. Wayne thought it was the best hug he had ever had. But he didn't want to take advantage of Mikey. He'd been through a traumatic experience and needed his rest. He released Mikey, and the city boy reluctantly stepped back.

"Well, I had better get to the station and grab my forensics kit. I need to secure the scene and get any evidence bagged up."

"It's late. Can't you wait until morning?"

"I don't want to risk losing any evidence if it rains or the weather turns windy. Best I get it done now. Do you need anything before I go?"

"Um, maybe some towels?" Mikey said.

"In the cupboard next to the bathroom. Help yourself."

Mikey thanked him and headed into the bathroom to shower. Wayne was momentarily distracted by the thought of Mikey being naked and wet in the next room but quickly shook it off, not wanting to be a creeper. He gathered his stuff and headed to the 4WD, noticing it was well after midnight.

This was going to be a long night.

Chapter Thirteen

MIKEY HAD TROUBLE falling asleep, his mind was still racing after the shock of seeing the blazing inferno that used to be his barn, desperately trying to work out why anyone would be targeting him like this.

He tried to remember if he had been involved in any confrontations with anyone since he arrived in Cooper's Landing; anyone he might of accidentally offended or upset. Nothing came to mind. Certainly, nothing that would justify vandalism and a potentially deadly fire.

But one thing did keep popping up in his mind. That day at the community centre and the mysterious man in the bushes who ran away as soon as he was spotted. Could he be involved? Who was he? Why would he do these things? Mikey eventually fell asleep, exhausted, with no solid answers.

He eventually awoke to the smell of bacon. It was mid-morning and the sun was streaming brightly through the guest room's window. Mikey quickly washed up in the bathroom, got changed and followed his nose to the kitchen when he found Wayne sitting at the kitchen table reading the newspaper.

"Good morning. I was just about to come in and wake you." Wayne said, putting down the paper and handing him a triple shot latte in a Grinder Boys takeaway cup.

"No worries. Thanks for the spare room. The smell of bacon is much more welcome than the smell of burning rubble." Mikey sat down and moaned in appreciation as he took his first sip of precious caffeine.

Wayne stood and carefully removed a plate of bacon and eggs that was being kept warm in the oven, placed it in front of Mikey, then set about making some fresh toast.

"I'm not sure I can eat all of this. Like I've told you before, I'm a pretty light eater in the morning."

"Well, you better eat what you can. You're going to need all the energy you can get today."

"Why?"

"I have to take you into the station and conduct a formal interview with you. I need to gather as much information about this case as I can. A broken window is one thing, but last night someone could have been killed. I need to get to the bottom of all this right now."

Mikey felt a cold chill run through him at the thought of just how close he had come to death. If he hadn't been out with Wayne that night, he most likely would have stayed at home, gone to bed early and slept through the fire – possibly dying of smoke inhalation or burning to death if the fire had spread. It was sheer luck that someone spotted the smoke and called the Rural Fire Service before the whole property was destroyed.

"I'll tell you everything I know, not that I know that much. I don't understand why this is happening."

"Don't worry," Wayne said, placing his hands on Mikey's shoulders and giving them a supportive squeeze, "We're going to figure this out together."

~

"You think I'm responsible?" Mikey asked, incredulously.

Mikey had been sitting in the police station's interrogation room with Wayne for almost two hours, answering the same questions over and over and his patience was starting to wear thin. But when Wayne point-blank asked him if he had set fire to his own barn, he snapped.

"Of course not, but officially I have to ask," Wayne said, trying to calm him down.

"Why the hell would I burn down my barn? That doesn't make any sense!"

"There are plenty of reasons why someone would do that. An insurance payout perhaps?"

"That's where you're wrong. The barn isn't insured."

Wayne looked at him aghast.

"You don't have insurance?"

"Not on the outer buildings, no. Just on the main house. When I bought the ranch, I'd intended to get a structural engineer to come out and examine the outer buildings. I wanted to know if they were worth saving or not. But when I saw them up close for myself, I could tell it wouldn't be worth the money, and I saw no point in insuring a bunch of uninhabitable, dilapidated shacks that were only going to have to get demolished anyway."

"But they haven't been demolished."

"Well, no. I haven't got around to it yet."

"Why not?"

"Well, it wasn't a priority. They've been slowly disintegrating for half a century, so what's the rush? Besides, I wanted to paint them first."

"Paint them?" Wayne looked confused.

"Yeah. Set against the backdrop of the rest of the ranch, those old structures are quite beautiful in their own way. I wanted to capture them on canvas before I got rid of them. I only just finished the painting a few days ago. I can show it to you if you like."

"You can show me later when I drive you home," Wayne said, smiling, and Mikey felt his earlier anger drain away.

"It's funny," Mikey said, "Whoever burned down the barn sort of did me a favour. They've saved me the cost of demolishing it."

"I don't find anything funny about arson," Wayne said sternly, his brows furrowed.

"No, I didn't mean funny ha-ha. I just meant whoever did it clearly didn't know I was going to demolish the barn. If they had, they probably wouldn't have bothered."

Wayne appeared to give this some thought. Mikey took another sip of the coffee that Wayne's assistant Shirl had brought him a few minutes earlier. Wayne had chastised her for interrupting a formal interview, but Shirl had reprimanded him, reminding him that Mikey was his boyfriend, not a criminal. Wayne had blushed and Mikey had smiled when Shirl had left the room with a wink.

"I'm beginning to think that whoever is behind these attacks isn't a local," Wayne said eventually, "Nobody in Cooper's Landing would start a fire, especially in the middle of bushfire season. Everyone knows how dangerous that is. And I haven't been able to get a single lead on the broken window incident. Nobody in town has heard anyone expressing homophobic views. Something tells me whoever wrote that note isn't the type to keep their opinions to themselves."

"So, where do we go from here?"

"Have you noticed anyone unusual hanging around the ranch? Any unexpected visitors? Door-to-door salesmen? People looking for work?"

"No nothing like that…" Mikey suddenly remembered the strange lights at night he had seen from the kitchen window. He told Wayne about them but wasn't sure they were related. The lights were way off in the distance, not near the ranch.

"Could be bushwalkers in the national park. Or maybe kids playing?" Wayne said, taking notes. Mikey wasn't convinced people did a lot of bushwalking at night, much less kids playing at night in the middle of nowhere. But he let it drop for the moment.

"Hey, I just realised. You're not in uniform. Shouldn't you be in uniform if you're on duty?"

Wayne smiled, "Technically, today is my day off. A relief officer from Bushman's Pass takes over two weekends a month and sleeps in the watch house. Otherwise, I'd be on call 24/7. Even super amazing hero cops like me have to have time off, ya know."

"Dork," Mikey laughed, "So where is this relief officer, then?"

"He's currently out on highway patrol, but he'll probably check in at some point today."

"But you're still working?" Mikey said, hating the idea of Wayne using what little time off he got on working his case.

"Yeah, because I'm the duty officer and this is *my* case. But don't worry. We're just about done here. I'll just hand this paperwork and audio recording over to Shirl, then we can get out of here."

Mikey felt a massive wave of relief come over him. Being interrogated was not fun. Even by a certain hunky country cop. So much for that fantasy.

Wayne offered to drive him home, but Mikey asked to be dropped off at Grinder Boys. He needed more coffee and to do some shopping. Besides, Wayne looked absolutely wiped out. He couldn't have gotten any sleep when he got home from doing the forensics work at the ranch. It was better if Wayne went home and got some rest. They could spend some time together later. Mikey also needed to air out the house and make sure the fire didn't cause any other damage to the property.

Wayne pulled up in front of the cafe, gave Mikey a soft, delicate kiss goodbye, then drove off.

~

"Do you have cheesecake? Please tell me you have cheesecake!" Mikey almost whined as he approached Sean at the counter.

"We have Triple Chocolate Cheesecake, why?"

"Gimme a huge slice and don't be stingy with the whipped cream."

"Oh dear, someone's eating their feelings. Did the big date go badly?" Sean asked, smiling, as he pulled out the cheesecake from the display cabinet and started plating up a slice.

"It was fine until the fire brigade showed up."

Scott appeared from the kitchen, "Really? That sounds hot!" he said with a cheeky grin and a wink.

"A little too hot. Someone burned down my barn last night."

Scott's immediately dropped his lecherous smile and moved to examine Mikey closely.

"Are you hurt, boy?" Scott said sternly, but Mikey could tell the older man was genuinely concerned.

"I'm fine, I just don't understand why this is happening to me. Have you guys ever had any trouble like this since you moved to town?"

"No, never," Sean said as he placed the cheesecake down in front of Mikey. The sumptuous treat was piled with whipped cream, chocolate sauce and fresh strawberries. Mikey immediately ate a forkful and groaned his appreciation. Sean returned to the table with a cup of coffee.

"How did you know I'd want coffee too?" Mikey said as he took a sip of the divine liquid.

"You're awake," Sean snarked playfully.

"Is that another triple shot?" Scott scowled disapprovingly.

"Leave the boy alone," Sean admonished his partner, "He's been through a trauma. A little coffee won't hurt him."

"A little coffee..." Scott muttered under his breath, "It's not healthy."

"If it makes you feel better, Scott, I've significantly cut back on my coffee drinking since I moved to Cooper's Landing. Back in the city, I'd go through at least four or five of these bad boys a day."

Scott's aghast expression at this disclosure was hilariously disproportionate; as if Mikey had just confessed to chronic methamphetamine addiction rather than a coffee habit. Mikey couldn't hold back his laughter as Scott started scowling again.

"I have work to do out the back," Scott grumbled as he stood and returned to the kitchen. Mikey suddenly felt bad for laughing at the man. It was clear Scott genuinely cared about him.

"Don't mind him," Sean said quietly, "He's a little sensitive about health matters. Ever since we lost Luke... well, he's become a little overprotective when it comes to people he cares about."

Mikey's soul ached for these two men. Although they had moved on with their lives, the pain they carried with them was still fresh. He was fortunate to have them as friends and his heart melted a little knowing that Scott, the big gruff Dom, was so sensitive to his safety.

"There must be an explanation to all this," Sean said, clearly wanting to change the subject, "Maybe whoever is doing this thinks you're somebody else?"

"Mistaken identity?" Mikey said, giving this some thought, "I don't think so. The ranch has been vacant for decades before I moved in. Besides, I think someone is following me around. I saw this guy in the bushes at the community centre the other day, and he ran off as soon as I spotted him."

It was Sean's turn to look aghast.

"Following you? Are you certain?"

"I don't know. There's also these weird lights on my property at night. Far off in the distance, near the national park. Wayne reckons it's bushwalkers or kids mucking about, but I'm not so sure. Seems more like somebody is creeping about in my back paddocks. But why? There's literally nothing there."

"I don't like you being out there on your own. I think you should come and stay with us. At least until all this is straightened out."

"I appreciate the offer, but I'm not going to be run out of my own home. Wayne will catch whoever's doing this soon."

"I know how you feel, but don't be stubborn," Sean said, sounding more like his partner.

"Huh! Good luck with that!" a familiar voice said from behind them. Mikey turned to see Wayne walking into the cafe.

"Hello, stranger. Long time no see!" Mikey said with a smirk.

"Now I see why you only ate a little bit of breakfast this morning. You were saving room for cheesecake." Wayne smirked back.

"Hey, this is medicinal! I've had a very stressful day." Mikey protested.

"I'll leave you boys to it," Sean said with a smile and discreetly returned to his position behind the counter.

"So, what are you doing back here? I thought you were going to get some sleep."

"I was, but I kept thinking about those lights on your property you mentioned earlier. Wouldn't hurt to check it out while it's still daylight. Fancy tagging along?"

"Sure. Just let me do one thing." Mikey said, downing the remainder of his coffee and standing.

He walked behind the counter and, with a reassuring nod from Sean, went into the kitchen area. Scott was standing by the large industrial sink, washing dishes. The big man didn't make any move to turn around when Mikey approached him.

"Scott?"

Scott gruffly grunted in response, continuing with his work. Mikey put his arms around Scott's waist, resting his head between the older man's enormous shoulders, giving him a tight hug from behind.

"Thanks for looking out for me. I appreciate it."

Scott stiffened momentarily but relaxed into the embrace.

"You're welcome, boy," he said quietly.

Mikey released him and left Scott to his dishes.

Chapter Fourteen

BY THE TIME Wayne and Mikey made it out to the Riverside Ranch, it was mid-afternoon and the heat of the day was at its most intense. Wayne had quickly changed into light, airy clothes before meeting up with Mikey, knowing he would be doing some hiking, and suggested Mikey change into something similar.

While Mikey got changed, Wayne went into the kitchen and packed some bottled water and a few snacks into his backpack. He didn't anticipate them being out for too long, but he didn't want to be caught without basic supplies in an emergency. He quickly checked his police-issue sidearm, ensuring it was loaded, and clipping it into the holster on his hip.

When his hiking partner emerged, wearing a lightweight t-shirt and cargo pants, Wayne handed him a broad-brimmed hat and some sunscreen. The harsh, blistering heat outside meant they needed all the protection they could get. Once the sunscreen was applied, the two men headed out the back door, down the porch stairs and across what had decades ago been the ranch yard.

Mikey took a moment to survey the burned rubble of the old barn. All that remained was a pile of charcoal, ashes and twisted metal. Wayne hadn't found much in the way of useful forensic evidence. He had collected the various fuel cans that had been left strewn around the area, but he held out little hope of getting any fingerprints or DNA from them, given their burnt condition. The relief officer at the station would take the retrieved evidence up to Bushman's Pass for examination at the end of his duty shift.

"Come on, we should make a move," Wayne said, and Mikey nodded his agreement, turning away from the debris.

"Couldn't we drive?" Mikey asked after a few minutes of walking, "You've got a four-wheel drive, after all."

"The old service road that runs the length of the property is overgrown and hasn't been maintained in decades. I don't want to end up hitting a fallen tree or something. The paddocks are overgrown too and could be hiding anything from exposed rocks to land subsidences. It's not safe to drive over either."

"Jeez, what did I buy?" Mikey said, sounding a little disturbed.

"It wouldn't be so bad if the land had been maintained over the years, but it's just been left to rot. It would take a lot of time, work and money to make this a functional ranch or farm again. Now you know why it was sold for so cheap."

"Well, thankfully I'm not planning on doing anything like that. I don't think I'm the farmer type. I'd look terrible in dungarees." Mikey chuckled to himself. Wayne shook his head, amused at the city boy's complete lack of country knowledge.

As they continued their trek along the badly decomposed service road, its dry compacted surface barely visible through the years of neglected weeds that now covered it, the heat of the day was punishing. Wayne pulled out a couple of bottles of water and handed one to Mikey. They took a quick rest as they slicked their thirst. Mikey pulled a large red handkerchief out of his back pocket and used it to wipe the sweat away from his face and neck. He then placed it around the back of his neck, covering his exposed skin, and tied it loosely around his throat.

As he surveyed the road ahead, Wayne was beginning to have second thoughts about their little afternoon hike. They'd been out there for almost an hour and were still nowhere near the northern boundary. They would start to lose light soon and he didn't want to be staggering around in the dark, especially in such unfamiliar and unsafe territory.

Also, as irrational a feeling as it was, he was beginning to suspect that they weren't alone out there. Between the tall grass and the various wild shrubs that lined the eastern boundary, there were plenty of places that someone could conceal themselves. He refused to mention that to Mikey. He didn't want to unnecessarily frighten the man with what was, in all probability, unfounded suspicions. But Wayne couldn't deny the tiny hairs standing up on the back of his neck.

"Maybe we should leave it for today. It's a lot hotter than I was expecting and we only have a couple of hours of daylight left," Wayne said.

"Yeah, it's pretty harsh. Why don't we look around for another twenty minutes, and if we don't find anything, we'll turn around and head back."

"Agreed."

The two men searched around the immediate area, not entirely sure what they were looking for. Wayne wasn't even sure if there was anything for them to find if he set aside his paranoid feelings. He was beginning to think this whole trip was a complete waste of time.

"Wayne! Look at this!" Mikey called out from a short distance ahead. Wayne ran over and looked at the ground where Mikey was pointing. The dry dirt of the road had been disturbed.

"Those look like tyre tracks," Mikey said.

"Too small to be a car or farm equipment. Maybe a trail bike or an ATV."

"So someone *has* been out here."

"Apparently so. Though I can't think why. Besides your house, there's nothing around for miles. Maybe it's kids hooning around on dirt bikes?"

"I don't think so. It's a bit far from town."

Wayne had to agree, it wasn't very likely. He touched one of the tracks, disturbing the lightly packed dust easily, "These tracks are pretty recent. Are you sure you haven't heard any bikes or engines at night?"

"No, and I'd be able to hear something like that clearly from the house. It's so quiet out here at night, the slightest noise carries. In fact,

I often have to put music on at night to get to sleep. I'm just so used to the noise of the city."

Wayne chuckled at that. He couldn't imagine becoming so accustomed to constant noise or finding silence off-putting. He'd grown up in the country, and the peace and tranquillity of the bush was all he knew.

"Well, I think we should head back now. At least we know someone has been out here recently. We can conduct a proper search tomorrow."

Wayne and Mikey packed the empty water bottles away and made their way back down the dirt track toward the ranch. It was after five when they finally returned to the house. Wayne unpacked the backpack and disposed of the empty bottles while Mikey put the uneaten snacks away.

"I was thinking of cooking dinner tonight," Mikey said, "I wanted to try out a new recipe. Would you care to be my taste tester?"

Wayne liked the idea of that, but he stank of dry sweat from their hike and he hadn't thought to bring a change of clothes. He was also tired, having not slept since the night before. But Mikey's expression was so hopeful, he couldn't say no.

"I'll need to head home and get a change of clothes first."

"No worries, I can start cooking while you freshen up. Be back here in an hour?"

"Sure. But I'll have to make it an early night. I need to get some rest."

"You could spend the night here. With me." Mikey blushed and looked away, as if embarrassed. It was adorable.

"Something tells me I wouldn't get much rest if I did that." He chuckled, "Maybe we could do that another time, but dinner is a definite yes."

Mikey smiled sweetly, although Wayne could tell the city boy was a little disappointed. But he could also tell that Mikey understood and didn't take his refusal as a rejection – just a raincheck. He leaned in and gave Mikey a gentle kiss, playfully biting his bottom lip, which earned him a groan that went straight to his groin.

The two men walked out to the front porch but were stopped in their tracks when they saw Mikey's ute. The vehicle had the words "LAST CHANCE" spray-painted in large, black letters, while the windscreen had the words "GET OUT" scrawled across it.

"My car! You've got to be fucking joking!" Mikey roared with anger.

Wayne couldn't believe it. They hadn't been gone much more than two hours. Whoever did this was ballsy, given there was a police vehicle parked only a few metres away.

"Who the hell is doing this? This is bullshit!" Mikey was livid.

Wayne saw a slight movement amongst the overgrown bushes that stood between Mikey's front yard and the road. A figure in dark clothes was attempting to hide in the scrub.

"Stay here!" Wayne hissed at Mikey. He drew his sidearm and ran toward the figure, who immediately darted away toward the road.

"Police! Don't move!" Wayne yelled out. The figure ignored him and continued to run. Wayne gave chase, easily catching up to the mysterious assailant who was obviously not as fit as Wayne was. The figure dressed in dark suddenly tripped on a rock and hit the ground like a tonne of bricks. Wayne caught up quickly and stood over the man, in his forties, who was now desperately out of breath.

Wayne aimed his weapon at the man and the suspect raised his hands slowly, surrendering peacefully.

"You're not going to give me any trouble, are you?" Wayne asked.

"No, please! Don't shoot!" the man said in a shaking, breathless voice.

Wayne quickly handcuffed the suspect and was dragging him to his feet when Mikey caught up to them.

"Is everything okay?"

"I told you to stay at the house!" Wayne admonished.

"I was worried about you."

"Do you recognise this guy?"

Mikey took a long look at the suspect. "He's the guy from the community centre. But I have no idea who he is. But... he does seem familiar from somewhere," Mikey said, looking puzzled. Wayne started to search the suspect and quickly found a can of spray paint in the front pocket of his hoodie.

"You're under arrest."

The suspect looked at the ground and elected to say nothing further. As Wayne loaded him into the back of the 4WD and told Mikey that unfortunately, they would have to postpone their dinner date while he processed the prisoner, a look of resolve crossed Mikey's face.

"Not so fast. I'm coming too." Mikey said.

"What? No, I need to..."

"I need to know who the fuck this guy is and why he's been targeting me. I need answers, Wayne. I'm sick of sitting on the sidelines with this. I'm coming with you." he said with finality.

And with that, the city boy jumped into the front passenger side seat and buckled up. Wayne had to admire Mikey's determined attitude and decided to let him tag along to the station. Mikey was right. He deserved answers. Hopefully, Wayne would be able to get some for him.

Chapter Fifteen

MIKEY SAT DOWN at Wayne's desk in the back of the police station and watched on as the mystery man, who had been causing so much trouble in his life, was processed by another police officer.

The younger cop, who Wayne introduced as Constable Simon Tran, had arrived only a few minutes after Wayne had radioed him to return to the station. Their prisoner was quickly searched, fingerprinted and taken to the lone interview room while Shirl, an older woman with outrageous iridescent green eyeshadow and wearing a bright orange and purple kaftan, ran a background check using the prisoner's drivers license found in his wallet.

Mikey wanted answers. He *needed* answers. He had to know who this guy was and why he had been harassing him ever since he first arrived in Cooper's Landing.

But there was something odd about the whole situation; something Mikey couldn't quite put his finger on. The mystery man seemed strangely familiar, but he couldn't figure out where he knew him from. Aside from their brief encounter at the community centre, Mikey was fairly certain he had never seen the man before. And yet, he was sure he knew him.

Then there were his actions. Breaking windows and sending threatening notes is one thing; burning down a building is quite another. Such an escalation seemed a little extreme but, then again, Mikey still didn't know the man's motivations. Mikey couldn't imagine what he could possibly have done to justify all this.

After a few minutes, Mikey was broken from his thoughts when Wayne approached with a printout in his hand.

"According to his driver's license, the suspect has a Melbourne home address. James Arthur Dunbar..."

"Dunbar?" Mikey repeated, his voice barely a whisper. Realisation hit him like a tidal wave as several of the puzzle pieces fell into place in his head.

"Does the name sound familiar?" Wayne asked in his official tone.

"I can't believe I didn't put it together earlier." Mikey said, "Yeah, I know him. I've known him for years."

"Who is he?"

"He's my father's chauffeur," Mikey said through gritted teeth.

Mikey should have known his father would be behind all this. He knew the old bastard wouldn't let it go. Mikey was furious but somehow managed to keep his emotions in check.

"Your father sent his chauffeur all the way out here to harass you? What kind of parent does that?" Wayne asked, looking equally shocked and confused.

"The kind that hates not getting his way and the kind with the pathological need to get the last word – no matter what."

"Okay, back up a bit." Wayne said, sitting down opposite Mikey, "I think you need to fill me in on what exactly happened to make you leave Melbourne in the first place."

Mikey took a deep, steadying breath and began recounting his life story. He explained how he had never been given any choices in his life. How he was just required to follow the path his father had laid out before him. He told Wayne about Justin's death, and how it had been the catalyst for Mikey finally deciding to break free of his father's controlling grip and get as far away from Randall Bradshaw's influence as possible.

"But how come you didn't recognise Dunbar initially?" Wayne asked.

"That's simple. He was my father's chauffeur for years. But I only ever saw the back of his head. Occasionally I'd hear his voice, but it's not like we were best friends or anything."

"I guess that makes sense. So, you decided to resign and leave Melbourne?" Wayne asked, urging Mikey to continue his story.

"Once I'd resigned and started packing, my father was furious. He threatened to disinherit me if I didn't immediate come back to work. I told him to go right ahead and disinherit me. His money meant nothing to me and it still doesn't."

"I'm betting he didn't like that."

"You'd win that bet. He made one last attempt to bully me into changing my mind. On the night before I was due to leave Melbourne, my father sent his team of lawyers around to my home. Just to personally hand-deliver an updated copy of his will which I had now been officially removed from. I assume he thought I would immediately back down and come crawling back to him." Mikey said, shaking his head.

Once he had finished telling him his story, Wayne's eyes were wide as saucers. Clearly, he hadn't expected Mikey's father to be behind all this. Mikey silently chastised himself for not figuring out his father's involvement sooner.

Mikey was resolved. He had made a new life for himself in Cooper's Landing, and he wasn't going to let his father or anyone else spoil it. This nonsense would end now.

"May I borrow your phone while you question Mr Dunbar?" Mikey motioned to the landline on Wayne's desk, "I think it's time I spoke with my father."

"Why not use your phone?" Wayne asked, looking puzzled.

"Because I'm pretty sure he won't answer if he sees my number come up on the Caller ID."

"Ah, fair enough. Go ahead."

Mikey watched as Wayne walked into the interview room, closing the door behind him. He picked up the receiver and dialled the number for his father's 'special line' from memory, which would get him directly through to Randall Bradshaw's office, bypassing the company's switchboard and his father's sycophantic executive assistant. He knew from experience that his father only used the special line for the most important of clients, so wouldn't risk not answering – even if he didn't recognise the number.

"Randall Bradshaw."

"Mr Dunbar is under arrest," Mikey said cooly.

"Hello, Michael. That is unfortunate. But why tell me?"

"Well, he is your chauffeur, Father."

"Not any more. He handed in his resignation weeks ago. So I certainly can't be held responsible for his actions. Nor would I be interested in assisting him to get out of whatever criminal enterprises he's caught himself up in."

"How convenient."

"Yes, it is." his father said, smugly.

"He's facing some serious charges, Father. I can't believe you would actually go this far. Seriously, are you that desperate to get your way?"

"I have no idea what you're talking about. Now if you'll excuse me, Michael, I have a lot of work to do."

"Damn it, Father! This isn't some game. He burned down a building, for God's sake! People could have been killed. What the hell are you playing at?"

Randall Bradshaw was suddenly silent.

"This ends right now. I'm not returning to Melbourne. My life is here now. So back off, or I will make you very, very sorry." Mikey said with arctic coldness.

"Are you threatening me, Michael? You know that's a criminal offence, don't you?" Randall chuckled.

"Well, you would know all about criminal offences, wouldn't you Father. Like that deal last year with Corona Industries?"

His father went silent again.

"Oh good!" Mikey said with mock glee, "I have your attention."

"I don't know what you think..."

"Did you really think I would leave the company without some kind of an insurance policy? I have copies of all the files pertaining to the Corona deal. They're currently being held by my lawyers, with additional copies held in multiple safe deposit boxes. So here's what's going to happen. You're going to back off and never contact me again in any way, shape or form. And if anything happens to me, my house, my property, or even if one of my windows gets so much as a smudge on it – my lawyers have strict instructions to forward the files directly to the Australian Securities and Investment Commission."

Randall started spluttering, but Mikey wasn't done.

"By the time ASIC and the Federal Police are finished with you, your company will be a smoking crater, much like my barn, and you'll be in prison for securities fraud. Don't test me, Father. Remember who raised me."

With that, Mikey slammed the phone's receiver down with a satisfying thud and took a deep breath. Randall Bradshaw might be stubborn, but he wasn't stupid. Mikey knew that he wouldn't be having any further trouble from him. Not if his father wanted to avoid a lengthy prison term.

Wayne emerged from the interview room a few moments later looking frustrated. He sat down opposite Mikey, frowning deeply.

"Well, that was a waste of time. He wouldn't say a word. I couldn't even get him to confirm his identity."

"I had a bit more luck with my father. He didn't admit he sent Dunbar here, but he told me enough to ensure I *knew* that he had. On the upside, I don't think I need to worry about my father causing any further problems for me."

"Why? What have you done?" Wayne asked, his eyes narrowing.

It was then Mikey realised that being a police officer, his new beau may not be entirely impressed with the action he had just taken on the phone. Aside from the obvious legal issues, Wayne would probably be somewhat disturbed that Mikey was capable of such behaviour, no matter how justified. Mikey didn't want to have to take the nuclear option with his father, but he had always suspected that eventually, he'd have no choice.

"Oh, nothing…" Mikey said, trying for innocence.

"Mikey?" Wayne wasn't buying it.

"Um, well, hypothetically speaking, just how illegal is blackmail?"

"Very," Wayne said, not sounding impressed.

"What if we called it 'extortion' instead?" Trying for levity.

"Equally as illegal!"

"Well then," Mikey said with a smile, "Lucky it's just a hypothetical."

Wayne just sat there, glaring at him sternly, his arms crossed. Mikey suspected this was his technique for cracking perps. It was working. Mikey needed a distraction.

"So, Dunbar won't talk, huh?" Mikey asked, desperately wanting to change the subject, "Mind if I have a word with him?"

"What? He's a prisoner. I can't just…"

"Just give me five minutes alone with him. Trust me, I can get him to talk. I'll even leave the interview room door open."

Wayne looked at him with a stern expression, clearly trying to decide if this was a good idea. After a moment, he reluctantly agreed. Mikey went into the interview room and sat down opposite Dunbar.

The older man looked deflated but nervous. It was obvious something had gone horribly wrong with his plan – and being under arrest in a country cop shop wasn't part something he had anticipated.

"Mr Dunbar," Mikey said in greeting, keeping his expression neutral.

"I'm not saying anything to you."

"You don't need to. You only have to listen. I've just spoken with my father, and he won't be bailing you out. He won't be sending his fancy, high priced lawyers. He's washed his hands of you and thrown you under the bus."

Dunbar's eyes widened but he said nothing.

"You're facing some pretty serious charges, you know that, right? The vandalism is petty and barely worth the court's time. But the arson? What the hell were you thinking? Burning down my barn during bushfire season? People could have died. Why did you do it?"

Dunbar went pale and started shaking.

"I don't know what you're talking about!"

"Oh, come on. It's over. You're facing attempted murder charges over this, and my father isn't going to help you. The best thing you can do is tell your side of the story and plead for mercy."

"But... But... I didn't do anything like that!" Dunbar said desperately, "Arson? Attempted Murder? All I did was break a window and spray paint your ute. Followed you around a bit. I don't know anything about burning down a barn. He just wanted me to scare you so you'd go back home. I wouldn't start a fire, I swear! I want to speak with a lawyer."

Mikey stared at him for a moment, contemplating Dunbar's words. He'd confessed to the vandalism without a second thought, but the talk of arson seemed to genuinely shock him. Mikey had expected him to either deny everything or remain totally silent. After a moment, Mikey rose from his seat, left the interview room and rejoined Wayne at his desk.

"Anything?" Wayne asked with genuine curiosity.

"He's confessed to the vandalism, but denies burning down the barn."

"Big surprise! That's the most serious charge."

"I believe him."

"What?" Wayne sounded almost incredulous.

"He was just so shocked when I mentioned the arson. When he realised he was facing such serious charges, he began to panic and started talking. I'm pretty sure he didn't have anything to do with it."

"Well," Wayne said looking concerned, "That answers one question but brings up a new one. If Dunbar didn't burn down your barn, who the hell did?"

Chapter Sixteen

WAYNE WAS EXHAUSTED, having been awake almost two days straight, but thankfully he was almost ready to leave the station. He would complete the interview with Dunbar then leave Constable Tran to close up.

But with the revelation that Dunbar was likely not responsible for the fire at the Riverside Ranch, Wayne was hesitant about letting Mikey go home alone. Until the arsonist was identified and in custody, Mikey was still in danger. It was then he remembered that the city boy's ute was still at the ranch, and he had no way of getting back home, short of walking all the way out to the ranch.

This gave Wayne an idea.

"Mikey," he said, holding out his keys to the younger man, "Why don't you take my 4WD and head over to my place. I'll finish up here and be there in an hour. Shirl can give me a ride when she's finished her shift."

Mikey looked a little confused, "Is that a good idea? I know how tired you must be and..."

"Exhausted, but I'll sleep better knowing you're safe. You can stay with me until all of this is sorted out. We'll get some more of your stuff tomorrow, but right now I just want to eat and get a full night's sleep."

"Okay," Mikey agreed, "I'll order us some Chinese for dinner."

"City Boy!" Wayne laughed, shaking his head, "You'll only get Chinese food if you cook it yourself. The nearest Chinese restaurant is about two hundred kilometres away!"

"Oh, bugger. I didn't think of that." Mikey said, "I suppose pizza is out too, then?"

"The only way you get food delivered around here is if you have a baby or someone dies. Then you get inundated with casseroles."

"I'm not sure I'm ready to make that much of a commitment just to get dinner. I guess I'll have to improvise something. Be afraid, be very afraid!" Mikey said with a wicked gleam in his eye as he jangled the keys and walked out of the station. Wayne couldn't hide the smile on his face, which Shirl noticed immediately.

"You better keep an eye on that boy, Sarge. He's a keeper."

"Yeah," Wayne's smile faded, "Until he gets bored and heads back to the city."

"I dunno," Shirl said, "I reckon he'll fit in here just fine. Be patient. Give him some time to adjust."

~

Wayne completed the interview with Dunbar quickly. The man didn't hold anything back, his conversation with Mikey having made him a lot more cooperative. Wayne shuddered to think what the city boy had said. Not to mention that cryptic phone call with his father. Wayne wasn't sure he wanted to know about any of it.

Dunbar confessed to the vandalism and implicated Randall Bradshaw as being the one who paid him to come to Cooper's Landing with the express purpose of stalking and harassing Mikey. Unfortunately, without some kind of evidence that linked Bradshaw to all this, it was his word against Dunbar's.

He denied any knowledge or involvement with starting the fire at the ranch. Wayne had initially thought Dunbar was just trying to get himself off the hook for the most serious charges, but he was good at reading people. Dunbar may have been a petty thug, but he wasn't an arsonist.

The vandalism charges were hardly worth taking to court, so Wayne offered to let him off with a fine, strictly on the condition that Dunbar leave town that night and never return. He readily agreed, clearly wanting this business to be over. Dunbar was issued a field citation and released to collect his belongings from the pub, where he had been staying since he arrived in town, and arrange immediate transport out of town.

By the time Shirl dropped him off at his house, Wayne was ready to forget about everything and just relax. He really needed to find a way of getting Tran transferred here full time. He was starting to grow weary of being the only cop in town.

"Have a good night, love. Don't do anything I wouldn't do!" Shirl said wickedly, cackling like a witch as she drove away. Wayne just shook his head with amusement. The local gossips would be busy tonight, spinning any number of tall tales about romance and erotic encounters at the local cop's house. Wayne would be happy with just a hot meal and maybe some more kissing with a certain city boy.

As he stepped in the front door, Wayne was instantly hit with the aroma of garlic and bacon. He quickly removed his boots, removed his gun belt and secured his sidearm in the weapon's safe in his bedroom. Joining him in the kitchen, he found Mikey, who appeared to be preparing a more elaborate meal than had ever been prepared in Wayne's kitchen. Despite his best efforts, Wayne had never been much of a cook. He never really had the time. So if it couldn't be microwaved or served on a sandwich, he didn't eat it.

"Your kitchen is a joke." Mikey said as he stirred something on the stove, "I did my best, but you had virtually nothing to cook with. I managed to cobble together Spaghetti Carbonara with garlic bread. I would have done a side salad but, if your fridge is any indication, you're allergic to vegetables."

Wayne was gobsmacked. He couldn't believe Mikey, who had previously claimed not to be much of a cook either, had somehow managed to pull all this together.

"I'm astonished you were able to find enough ingredients to make even this. Thank you, but you didn't need to go to all this trouble."

"I did if I wanted to eat." Mikey said with a smile, "Why don't you go and wash up? This will be ready in about ten minutes."

Wayne moved up close behind Mikey, wrapped his arms around his waist and kissed him on the cheek, working his way down the city boy's neck. Mikey melted in his arms and let out a contented whimper that went straight to Wayne's cock.

"Be right back," he whispered in Mikey's ear, smiling as he noticed the city boy's shiver as Wayne's lips brushed his earlobe.

Wayne headed for the bathroom, stripped off and made quick work of showering. Once he was dry and changed into some casual clothes, he felt a thousand times more refreshed and relaxed. Knowing he wasn't on call that night was just the icing on the cake. He could wind down for the first time in days. Plus, having a handsome man in his home didn't hurt either.

~

"This is incredible!" Wayne said as he used some bread to mop up the last of the sauce off his plate. Mikey beamed at the praise, his smile wide enough to make his eyes crinkle at the corners.

"A few months ago, I could barely make toast. Now I'm making whole meals and impressing the masses with them. Thank God for the internet!" Mikey chuckled as he cleared the empty plates and deposited them in the sink.

"Why don't you join the masses over here on the couch. I think you've earned a rest."

The city boy didn't even hesitate. He simply put down the bottle of dishwashing liquid and joined Wayne on the couch, snuggling in when Wayne put his arm around him. Wayne loved the feeling of cuddling a handsome man on his couch and briefly lamented to himself about how infrequently he had experienced such a simple pleasure.

"This is nice," Wayne said as switched on the television and flicked through the channels, the two men finally settling on some old black and white movie. Mikey sighed in what Wayne believed was contentment as they settled in to watch the film.

"Can I ask you something?" Mikey asked when the end credits rolled, sitting up and facing Wayne.

"Anything."

"Are you really going to make me sleep in the guest room tonight?" he asked with a cheeky half-grin and fire in his eyes.

Wayne was instantly hard.

"No," Wayne said, "You can sleep on the couch if you like." a devilish grin on his face.

"Ha!" Mikey laughed and playfully slapped him on the arm, "Shut up and take me to your bed, already!"

"Gee, you city boys sure are bossy, ain't ya?"

"You better believe it!"

Wayne stood up, bent over and scooped Mikey up into his arms – the city boy squealing and giggling at the unexpected manhandling – and Wayne did as instructed. He carried Mikey out of the living room, down the hallway and into his bedroom, depositing him on the bed.

Wayne climbed on top of Mikey, putting all his weight on his arms, and brought their lips together in a scorching kiss. Mikey moaned, arching his hips up to meet Wayne's, grinding together slowly. Wayne thought he was going to lose his mind if the city boy kept that up.

"I never thought to ask before," Wayne said breathlessly, "Do you have any preferences?"

Mikey smiled shyly, "Yeah. My preference is for you to make love to me."

Wayne could live with that. He rolled over and brought Mikey with him, allowing the younger man to straddle his hips as they continued kissing. Wayne pushed his hands under Mikey's t-shirt and began exploring the man's smooth skin. He found his pert nipples and began teasing them gently with his thumbs, Mikey whimpering with pleasure.

Before long, the two men were naked and Wayne reached over to the bedside table for the lube and condoms. Before he could do anything else, Mikey slowly began licking his way down Wayne's torso until he reached his hips. The younger man gently nibbled at the sensitive flesh where his thigh met his groin, sending a ticklish sensation through Wayne.

"Tease!" Wayne hissed through his teeth.

But any further words were lost when Mikey took him into his mouth. Feeling his cock enveloped by that tight, wet heat made Wayne groan deeply with pleasure. He wanted to grab hold of Mikey's head and control the action but he resisted the primal urge. Instead, he watched as Mikey slowly bobbed up and down, his eyes never breaking contact with him. It was the sexiest thing Wayne had ever seen.

"If you want me to make love to you, you better stop that. Your mouth feels so fuckin' good."

Mikey pulled his mouth off of his cock with a pop, which damn near killed Wayne. The younger man's puffy lips, slick with spit and precum, quirked into a sly grin.

Mikey took some of the lube and began prepping himself, starting with a single finger, then adding two more in succession. Wayne quickly sheathed his manhood and positioned himself over Mikey, lining his cock up with Mikey's waiting entrance. He carefully pushed forward, watching for any sign of discomfort, but was relieved as Mikey nodded for him to continue. Soon, Wayne was all the way in, Mikey's tight passage squeezing him gently.

"Are you okay?" Wayne asked.

"Just give me a minute." Mikey panted, "You're a lot thicker than I expected."

"Do you want me to pull out?"

"No, I'll be okay."

Wayne kissed him, carefully massaging his tongue against Mikey's. He could feel Mikey relax and Wayne carefully drew back a little, then pushed forward again. Mikey's eyes were like fire.

"Please move again. I need you to move, Wayne!" he said, almost desperately. Wayne snapped his hips, plunging out then in sharply, hitting that sweet spot deep inside. Mikey cried out with pleasure.

Wayne increased his thrusting, building up to a steady pace. Mikey's hips began to move, meeting him thrust for thrust. Wayne knew he wouldn't last too long, Mikey's oral skills having left him a lot closer to the edge than he would have liked. He grabbed hold of Mikey's hard cock, now leaking a steady stream of precum, and began pumping it in time with their thrusts. Both men were panting as if the room were running out of air. Their hot, sweaty bodies were slapping together like wild animals. Wayne was barely keeping it together, but when he felt Mikey shudder, he watched as the younger man found his release. Wayne continued to fuck him until he too had gone over the edge. He quickly pulled out, disposed of the condom and rolled over to lay by Mikey's side as they both caught their breath.

After a few moments, Wayne grabbed a warm, damp washcloth from the bathroom and cleaned up himself and Mikey. After disposing of the cloth, he returned to the bed, spooned in behind Mikey and covered them both with the bedsheet. Within moments, they were both asleep.

Chapter Seventeen

MIKEY WAS AWOKEN from a contented sleep at four AM by the sound of Wayne's phone ringing. The cop was a light sleeper, so managed to answer the phone within two rings. A brief conversation later, Wayne hung up and he got out of bed and turned on the bedside lamp.

"What's happening?" Mikey asked, his eyes squinting at the sudden intrusion of light.

"That was Bushman's Pass station. They've asked me to assist with their narcotics task force. They need all hands on deck for a major operation."

Wayne quickly showered and dressed in a fresh uniform, removed his sidearm from the gun safe and collected his phone and keys from the bedside table. He leaned down and kissed Mikey softly and gently.

"I'm sorry about this. I'll be back as soon as I can, but I'll probably be all day."

"No worries. Go catch some bad guys." Mikey said with a sleepy grin, watching Wayne head out of the bedroom and down the hallway.

"I will!" Wayne called out as he left the house.

Mikey switched off the lamp and snuggled down in Wayne's warm, comfortable bed, surrounded by the scent of the man he was rapidly falling in love with. He slowly drifted back to sleep, Mikey's hole still throbbing deliciously from their passionate lovemaking earlier in the night.

When he woke up a few hours later, Mikey showered, dressed and scrounged up some toast and coffee. If he was going to be spending any more time at Wayne's house, Mikey would need to bring some essentials with him – such as decent coffee. The ancient can of cheaper than cheap instant coffee that Wayne kept in the kitchen cupboard tasted like dusty charcoal.

After breakfast, Mikey grabbed his things and locked the front door behind him. But without his car, a local taxi or even a ride share service – his only alternative was to walk. By car, the trip back to the ranch from Wayne's place would take ten minutes. On foot, it would take him about an hour. Thankfully, it was still early in the morning and the heat from the sun was mild at the moment.

About ten minutes into his long walk home, a white van pulled up on the side of the road ahead of him, honking its horn in a friendly tone. Mikey approached cautiously, not recognising the vehicle at first, but was pleased to see it was Travis driving. The muscular delivery man from the antique shop was smiling wide as he wound down the window.

"You need a lift, Mikey?"

"Actually, I wouldn't mind one, thanks."

"You going back to the ranch?" Mikey nodded, "Jump in. I'm heading out that way anyway."

Mikey opened the door, scrambled inside and put on his seatbelt. Travis carefully pulled out and they headed down the road toward the old highway.

"Looks like you had an interesting night," Travis said with a knowing smirk, "if that hickey on your neck is anything to go by."

Mickey blushed bright red and immediately adjusted his shirt in a lame attempt to cover the bruise on his neck.

"So, not just walking home, but doing the walk of shame, huh?"

"Oh no, there's no shame. I just didn't realise the hickey was that noticeable." Mikey chuckled. He would need to dig out his concealer when he got home before the entire town was gossiping about his night with Wayne.

"Well, good onya mate. I'm happy for you."

When they got to the ranch, Mikey invited Travis in for a cup of tea, but the younger man declined politely, saying he needed to get on to Bushman's Pass and make his deliveries. Mikey waved him off as the truck disappeared in a cloud of dust down the old unsealed driveway.

After changing his clothes and brewing up some coffee, Mikey set up his painting things on the back porch. Once the easel was set up, his favourite stool was in place and his paints ready to use, he sat down and started work on a new canvas. He started by using a small piece of charcoal to sketch the outline of the trees of the national park that dominated the horizon. The northern boundary of Mikey's property, which backed onto the rear of the national park, was marked by a rocky gully that was once the bed of the now diverted Gurangajin River.

This area also just happened to be the place where those mysterious lights had been appearing at night. Mikey put down the charcoal, distracted from his art by his deepening thoughts of everything that had been going on since his arrival. All the mysterious goings-on that had, for the most part, gone unexplained. The break-in the day after he moved in; The mystery lights outside at night; Dunbar's rock through the front window and vandalism of his vehicle; The barn fire; The tire tracks on the service road leading to the northern boundary.

With the exception of Dunbar's petty vandalism, which had been ordered by his father, Mikey couldn't explain any of the other incidents.

Wayne was right; the lights *could* be explained away as simply hikers near the national park or possibly kids riding trail bikes in the back paddocks. The tire tracks would seem to support the trail bike theory. But neither of these things seemed very plausible. Who went hiking or trail bike riding at night? Especially out in the middle of nowhere? Wouldn't Mikey have heard the engines of the trail bikes? They aren't exactly quiet, and it wasn't like there was the noise of heavy traffic nearby to cover the sound.

The barn fire was the thing that stood out most. Why burn it down? What was the purpose of that? Why not burn the house down instead? Even in the dark, someone with no knowledge of the ranch would recognise the difference between the two buildings. They would also realise the barn was a dilapidated old shack of no value. So burning it down made no sense.

Unless it was a message.

Was someone trying to tell Mikey something? Was burning down the barn supposed to send him a message? To make him back off from something? Maybe scare him away? If so, what was it that they wanted to keep hidden? The ranch and its surrounding property had stood empty for decades. There was literally nothing out there. The only thing of value, the river, had been diverted years ago. If someone wanted him gone, Mikey had no idea why.

The more he thought about it, the more Mikey became convinced that the northern boundary to his property appeared to be the key to solving everything. That's where the service road, where the tire tracks were found, lead to. That's where the mystery lights at night appeared to be coming from. If there were any answers to be found, Mikey would find them at the northern boundary.

He knew he shouldn't go out there alone. He knew he should wait for Wayne. But his curiosity got the best of him. Without a second thought, Mikey went into the kitchen and packed up the backpack with water, snacks and anything else he thought he would need. It was just before ten AM and according to his phone's weather app, the temperature was expected to be mild. While he wasn't exactly an experienced hiker, he knew he would still need some supplies on a long-distance trek. Once he had gathered everything he thought he would need, Mikey quickly pulled on his boots, broad-brimmed hat and the loaded backpack, then headed out the back door.

Before stepping off the porch, Mikey looked into the distance toward the national park. He couldn't see any signs of activity, but he had only ever seen the lights at night. He took a deep breath, descended the porch stairs and made his way toward the old service road. He predicted his trip to the northern boundary would take him at least two hours, possibly longer, depending on how badly blocked or degraded the service road was.

As it turned out, the road wasn't nearly as bad as Mikey had expected. There were a couple of fallen trees and a lot of overgrowth, but for the most part, the service road was passable. While he walked, Mikey had noticed various tire tracks in the ground. They crisscrossed each other and appeared to be of various ages. It seemed there was a lot of activity out here and had been for quite some time. But who would come out here and why? So far, Mikey had seen nothing remarkable except the scenery.

After about ninety minutes, Mikey was close to what had once been the site of the river but was now a craggy gully that separated his land from the national park. A natural rise in the land made him instinctively duck down and crawl toward the crest so he could get an unobstructed view of the dry riverbed that lay beyond while remaining out of sight. Of course, Mikey didn't think there was anyone out here to *see* him, but he didn't want to take any chances.

He peeked over the edge and looked down to see the wide stony gully that was once held the mighty Gurangajin River. Mikey's eyes widened when he saw what appeared to be a large storage shed that had been build near the riverbank. The structure, about two hundred metres from his position, was a complete surprise to him given that Mikey had not been told about any buildings being present on this part of the property. It certainly didn't appear on any of the site maps or aerial photos that he had seen.

Mikey looked around the surrounding area and didn't see anybody around. There were no sounds or evidence that there was anyone in or near the shed. On the other side of the gully, there was nothing but dense bushland and scrub leading up to the national park. The place was deserted.

The shed was enormous, big enough to hold at least three cars, but was completely hidden from view by a combination of the natural topography of the land and what appeared to be some very clear attempts to camouflage the structure. The corrugated iron walls of the shed had been painted natural earth tones to match the surrounding land. The roof was covered with strapped down tarpaulins that were covered in twigs, bark and dead leaves. From above, the shed would be indistinguishable from the surrounding scrub. Someone was clearly trying to hide something.

Deciding to take a closer look, Mikey slowly and carefully made his way toward the shed. He followed what appeared to be more old tire track marks down the embankment. Up close, the shed looked even bigger. On the far side, there was some kind of engine, possibly a generator. It too was camouflaged. Wires were leading from the generator into the shed. On the side closest to the riverbed, Mikey found a large sliding door. It was closed and locked with a large, sophisticated combination padlock, the kind that you would need bolt cutters to remove. The padlock was reasonably new looking, as was the shed itself. The paint job on the walls and sliding door, which up close Mikey discovered had also been crudely thatched with twigs and leaf matter, made it difficult to judge how long the shed had been there. But it was clear the structure was much more modern than any of the other buildings on the property and had been disguised to ensure nobody would see it from a distance.

Mikey looked around, but couldn't find another way into the shed, or even a crack to peek at the contents. He looked at the heavy padlock on the door and sighed. Up until this point, he had been holding on to the hope that the real estate agent had simply forgotten to mention this building. But the heavy and probably very expensive security lock was not the kind of thing a real estate agent would use to lock up a garden shed, and it certainly hadn't been out here since the last time anyone lived on the ranch. Someone was squatting on his land, and they clearly wanted to keep their activities and presence a closely guarded secret.

His blood ran cold. In that instant, he realised that coming out there alone was probably the most foolish thing he could have done. Nobody knew he was there. He had no backup. He was out of his depth and needed to get the hell out of there – now. Mikey took a quick look to see if the coast was clear, then quickly headed back up the embankment. Once he reached the hidden crest where he had been a few minutes earlier, he heard what sounded like rustling noises coming from the direction of the national park. Mikey ducked down and remained perfectly still. After a minute or so, the noise stopped. He smiled to himself. The wind was blowing the branches in the trees across the riverbank. He was allowing his imagination to run away with him.

Mikey lifted his head slightly only to quickly drop it back down against the ground again. Over the crest, down near the shed, stood a tall, bulky man facing away from Mikey.

He was dressed in camouflage gear, a broad-brimmed hat with dark mosquito netting that covered his face, and heavy combat boots. He appeared to be surveying the area, looking for something... or someone. Mikey quickly took another peek and forcibly held in his gasp as he saw the man turn around. Mikey crouched back down, forcing his face onto the dry, sandy earth. The man was holding what appeared to be some kind of semi-automatic machine gun.

Praying the gunman hadn't seen him, Mikey remained still and silent. Despite not being able to see the man's face, there was something vaguely familiar about him. His bulky physique and the way he moved. He couldn't be certain, but Mikey had a feeling he had met the gunman somewhere before. So if he had been spotted by the mystery man, Mikey was as good as dead.

He didn't have time to hang around. Mikey needed to get back to civilisation and report what he had discovered. He needed to tell Wayne everything and pray he wouldn't kill him for doing something so foolishly dangerous as hiking off into the middle of nowhere by himself.

He slowly and carefully backed away from the crest, not turning around or raising himself above a crouch. He quietly backed up until he was far enough away from the riverbank that he couldn't be observed from the gunman's position. He then quickly and quietly headed back to the service road, trying to stay out of sight as much as possible.

Mikey felt the hairs on the back of his neck stand on end. He imagined there were gunmen everywhere, hiding behind the trees and amongst the overgrown scrub. He shrugged off the feeling and kept moving. But the image in his mind of the gunman continued to haunt him, and would until he reached safety.

Chapter Eighteen

"ARE YOU INSANE?" Wayne roared after Mikey told him he had hiked out to the northern boundary of his property by himself. Wayne had returned home from Bushman's Pass earlier than expected to find Mikey gone. He decided to head out to the ranch, only to find Mikey running toward the house from the back paddock, out of breath and panicked. Once he'd had a chance to calm himself, Mikey had recounted the events of the morning.

"How could you do something so fucking reckless?" Wayne was beyond furious, "Typical city boy! I know you didn't grow up out here, but rule number one *and* two of hiking is *never* go hiking alone and *never* go hiking without telling someone where you're going. What if you had broken your leg? Or fallen down a gully and knocked yourself unconscious? With no way to call for help and nobody knowing where to look for you?"

Wayne was angry, but mostly he was terrified. He cared about Mikey and didn't want anything to happen to him. Just the thought of him being hurt or killed made Wayne's stomach turn. Wayne blamed himself for this. He should have explained the dangers to him better. Mikey was from the city and couldn't possibly know these things.

"I know," Mikey said sheepishly, "I'm an idiot. I shouldn't have done it. But I honestly didn't think I was in any danger. I brought water and supplies with me. I thought I'd be okay. I certainly didn't expect to come across some guy with a machine gun."

Wayne reined in his anger. Lecturing Mikey wasn't going to help the situation and he needed to get as much information out of him as possible. The younger man was obviously scared and contrite, but Wayne needed him relaxed. Mikey's discovery could be the break in the case he'd been desperately hoping for.

"Next time," Wayne said in a calmer tone of voice, "Let me know if you plan on doing something like that. Don't go off on your own. Now, tell me all about this shed you found. Something about it seems suss."

Mikey recounted everything he saw in detail, including the camouflaging and high-end security padlock. Alarm bells began to ring in Wayne's head. He had a bad feeling the barn fire was just the tip of the iceberg; that they were dealing with something a lot more serious than a simple act of arson.

"It's probably nothing. It's probably just some survivalist. You know, those nutters who live off the grid and don't want contact with the outside world? Maybe he's a doomsday prepper? Maybe he's homeless and he built the shed to live in, not knowing it was on private property?"

"Somehow, I doubt any of those suggestions explain what you saw. I'll admit, we occasionally get itinerant homeless people pitching their tents in the national park, but nothing like what you're describing. Besides, wandering around in camouflage gear with a machine gun? That seems a bit extreme."

"I guess. Plus the shed is enormous. I doubt it was built with human habitation in mind. What could it be for?"

Wayne had a bad feeling he knew exactly what the shed was for. He asked Mikey to pull out his laptop and open up the Maps application. They searched for a satellite image of the local area and focused in on the Riverside Ranch and the surrounding properties.

"So, where about's was this shed?" Wayne asked, pointing to the map on the laptop screen. Mikey gestured toward the dry riverbed, near the rear of the national park.

"Hmm, interesting choice of location," Wayne muttered to himself.

"Is it?"

"This satellite image was taken last year. The shed isn't there. Camouflaging doesn't make something invisible, just less noticeable.

But even zoomed in there's nothing there. So, we can conclude the shed must have been build recently, or at least since this image was taken."

Mikey looked like he was mulling something over in his head. His brow was furrowed as he stared at the image on the screen.

"What is it?" Wayne asked gently.

"Someone's trying to scare me off my land."

"What makes you say that?"

"Think about it. Think about everything that's happened since I arrived in Cooper's Landing. Whoever build this shed probably built it when the ranch was still unoccupied. They probably chose this property because it's isolated. And something tells me this isn't just one person. There's gotta be more people involved." Mikey stands up and starts pacing as he thought out loud.

"Anyway, the shed is huge and I doubt it's filled with flowers and puppies. It's gotta be something illegal. So they build their shed, use trail bikes and the cover of darkness to do whatever they're doing out there..."

"The lights at night?" Wayne interjected.

"Exactly. Now, everything is going nice and smoothly for them. Then, out of nowhere, the house is getting renovated. It's sold quickly and I move in. Suddenly their cozy, isolated, private little spot in the middle of nowhere isn't quite so private anymore."

"But who are 'they' in all this?" Wayne asks.

"I don't know. But clearly they weren't happy about me showing up. The first thing they did is break into my house the day after I moved in so they could search through my stuff. They were probably looking to find out who I was and where I'd come from. Before they can do anything though, someone throws a rock through my window with a threatening note attached."

"But we already know that was Dunbar," Wayne said.

"We know that now, but the shed people didn't. But they took full advantage of Dunbar's actions. They sat back and waited for him to scare me off for them. But it didn't work. I'm still here hovering over them. They know the longer I'm there, the more likely their little operation will be discovered. So that's when they decided to take matters into their own hands."

"Burning down the barn?"

"Yes. They don't even try to make it look like an accident. It sends a very clear message. But, once again, I don't leave. Now, I've stumbled upon their shed and seen one of them wandering around with a machine gun? It's only a matter of time before they decide to send another message."

Wayne started connecting dots in his mind. The vandalism; the barn fire; the mysterious shed; the recent increase in drug use both here and in Bushman's Pass. Everything lined up with his suspicions.

"I think I know what's going on with that shed and, if I'm right, you may have just unwittingly helped to solve Bushman's Pass Police's biggest case for them."

Mikey looked confused, "Case? What case?"

It was suddenly all so clear to Wayne. Mikey's discovery of the mysterious shed had proved to be the final piece of the puzzle. It's just the puzzle had turned out to be a lot larger than Wayne had initially realised.

"Remember when I told you Bushman's Pass has been having a lot of trouble with drugs recently? Specifically meth? Well, they keep arresting people, mostly users and low-level drug dealers, but they haven't been able to find the source. No stockpiles. No drug labs. Nothing. Worse still, they've tried setting up random roadblocks and still haven't been able to find any drugs being brought into town."

"You think they're making drugs in that shed?" Mikey asked.

"Or stockpiling them there. Or both. There may even be other sheds out there that we haven't found yet."

"Oh my god," Mikey breathed, "But, how are they getting them into Bushman's Pass then?"

Wayne pointed at the map on the laptop screen, "The dry riverbed. Remember the tire tracks you found? They might be using trail bikes or ATV's to transport the drugs down the riverbed, through the national park and out to the other side. See here?" he pointed to the abandoned highway.

"What is that?"

"Highway N44. They started building it years ago, but due to government funding cutbacks, it was never completed. It was almost finished, but the access roads connecting both ends to the existing roads were never put in place. But, the N44 is easily accessible from the northern end of the national park if you were to use a small off-road vehicle."

"Like a trail bike?" Mikey asked excitedly.

"Exactly. I think that's what's happening. We've got ourselves a group of drug runners, using your property, the dry river bed and the abandoned highway as the perfect way to get around the Bushman's Pass Police roadblocks and searches."

"But wouldn't someone in the national park notice all this? Park rangers?"

"More government cutbacks." Wayne said with frustration, "We haven't had a full-time park ranger in years. These days, the national park doesn't have any onsite staff at all. The rural fire service goes through the place once a month to make sure everything's safe as part of their fire reduction strategy, but that's about it."

Wayne grabbed his phone and started scrolling his contacts. He needed to contact Bushman's Pass Police immediately. He couldn't handle an operation of this scale single-handed. He would need some serious backup. But before he could place the call, Mikey stopped him.

"You realise what this means, right?" Mikey said, looking worried.

"Means?"

"Yeah. Everything you've just described. It all depends on some serious local knowledge of the area. No one from outside the area would be able to come up with something like this."

"What are you saying?" Wayne asked, but in his heart, he already knew what Mikey was going to say.

"I'm saying... someone here in Cooper's Landing has to be involved."

Chapter Nineteen

MIKEY'S HOUSE WAS a hive of activity by mid-afternoon, as police officers from Bushman's Pass began arriving at the Riverside Ranch to establish a command post. Arriving in unmarked vehicles and dressed in civilian clothes so as not to alert anyone in town to their prescience, the special tactical team and narcotics squad quickly unloaded their equipment in the living room and began preparing to converge on the mysterious shed at the northern end of the property.

Wayne briefed the senior officers on the situation, and it was agreed they would split into two teams; one small team that would seclude themselves within the national park, with the remaining officers heading out to the northern boundary and taking up positions around the shed. Once the people using the shed arrived on the scene, most likely after dark, the officers would move in, surrounding and detaining the suspects while executing a raid on the shed.

When Mikey first decided to leave the big city and settle in a small country town, he never imagined he would be the centre of a major police operation. He certainly never thought he'd have over a dozen police officers in his house dressed in bulletproof vests and carrying high powered automatic weapons. As he sat at the kitchen table, watching the officers make their preparations, Mikey's eyes rarely strayed from Wayne. This man that he cared so much for was about to enter a potentially deadly situation and Mikey was terrified that this may be the last time they ever see each other.

"Hey," Wayne said, joining Mikey at the table and breaking him from his worrying, "It's gonna be okay. These guys are the best. They've trained for this sort of thing and they'll get the job done."

"I know, but I'm still worried. What if something goes wrong. What if you get hurt or..."

"Sweetheart," Wayne reached out and held Mikey's face with both hands, gently caressing his cheeks with his thumbs, "This is what I do for a living. Admittedly, it's not usually this high-stakes, but I've been trained in tactical engagements. The whole point of these special teams is to reduce the likelihood of anyone getting hurt."

Mikey must not have looked convinced because Wayne smiled and swiftly pressed their lips together.

"Trust me."

"Okay, I trust you." Mikey smiled back, but he still felt scared inside. This was a dangerous situation.

"Mr Bradshaw, put this on." The senior tactical officer said, handing Mikey a bulletproof vest. Wayne looked both confused and angry.

"What's this for?" Mikey asked, equally confused.

"You're the only one who's seen this shed," the senior officer said, "You'll need to direct us since none of us know the exact position."

"Absolutely not!" Wayne roared, "He's a civilian! You can't seriously expect him to put himself in that kind of danger!"

"Time is of the essence, Sergeant Townsend, and it's likely the suspects believe their position has been compromised. We need to get into position ASAP. Otherwise, they may clear the shed out and move to a new location before we can secure the structure, its contents and the suspects."

Wayne and the senior tactical office continued to argue back and forth, while Mikey watched on. While Mikey was flattered that Wayne would jump to his defence, he had never seen the man act so aggressively before. It was both sexy and a little intimidating. But the arguing wasn't solving anything, and Mikey knew he needed to break the deadlock between them.

"Stop it! Both of you!" Mikey yelled at the top of his lungs. The entire house fell silent. "If anyone is interested in *my* opinion, I'm happy to lead the way."

"Mikey, that's not necessary..." Wayne began to argue, but Mikey cut him off by raising his hand.

"Wayne, I get that you're worried that I might get hurt, but he's right. Time is short. I can direct you all to the shed, then fall back to a safe spot while you all do whatever you have to do. I want this whole mess sorted out too, and if me showing you how to get to the shed helps to do that, then I'm willing to help."

If looks could kill, Mikey would have been a pile of ashes. Wayne was not happy with this plan, but eventually, he nodded and helped Mikey to strap the vest on.

"I don't like this." Wayne said as he adjusted the straps, "You shouldn't be doing this."

"I've got the vest on, plus I'll be surrounded by all these heavily armed cops. It's either this or we let the drug runners slip the net."

"Once we get close, you fall back. Just point us in the right direction then go. No hanging around. No dawdling. No heroics." Wayne said sternly.

"Yes, sir," Mikey said with a slight smirk.

"Now that I kinda like," Wayne smirked back. "But seriously, please be careful. I don't think I could bear it if anything happened to you."

The two men quickly hugged, then finished up their preparations. They would need to leave shortly to get into position before nightfall.

~

The first team departed in two unmarked cars, each driven by a plainclothes officer. The team of four tactical officers would be dropped off at the main entrance to the national park, then proceed on foot to their position near the boundary. The unmarked vehicles would then be driven away so as not to arouse any suspicion, should the drug runners use the same entry to the park.

The remaining tactical officers, plus Wayne and Mikey, departed the ranch at the same time, making their way on foot to the northern boundary via the old service road. The tactical officers were dressed in all black, with matching helmets, bulletproof vests and weapons.

Wayne and Mikey were dressed in dark clothes too, with Wayne donning a spare set of clothes he kept in his vehicle for just such an occasion. The two men were also issued radios with discreet earpieces, so they could remain in contact with the team.

Just as Mikey advised the senior tactical officer that they had reached the halfway point in their journey, the first team radioed in. They confirmed they were in position and had secluded themselves in the dense scrubland that boarded the national park. They had eyes on the shed, but there was no sign of activity or the gunman that Mikey had encountered earlier.

Time was almost up, but just as the sun was close to setting, the team was within spitting distance of the craggy gully where the shed was located. Mikey gave the senior officer the exact location as best as he could remember. The senior officer gathered his team around and issued them with their orders, including remaining totally silent until the order to move in was given. He also reminded them that if the suspects did show up, the tactical team were only to move in once the suspects had unlocked the shed. If they moved in too early, the suspects could deny their connection to the structure.

The team, including Wayne, quickly dispersed into their assigned positions. They secluded themselves with branches or lay flat on the ground amongst the long grass, waiting for the drug runners to make an appearance. Mikey watched as Wayne crouched down and lay himself close to where he himself had hidden from the gunman only a few hours earlier. He had never felt so nervous in his entire life.

"Mr Bradshaw," the senior officer whispered, "You need to remain here and keep low in the overgrowth. Do not move from this position until I or one of the team tells you to. Do you understand?"

"Yes, I do," Mikey whispered back. He crouched down in the long grass and watched as the senior officer quietly moved into his position.

There was nothing else to do now but wait. The sun was setting and the area was quickly being plunged into inky darkness. Normally,

Mikey found the nights in Cooper's Landing magical, but tonight it was oppressive and terrifying. He prayed that the operation would begin and end soon. If the drug runners didn't show up, then the tactical team might have to do this all again tomorrow. Mikey knew they weren't keen on just raiding the shed, since they wanted to catch the occupants as well.

As it happened, they didn't need to wait long. About an hour after sunset, Mikey heard through his radio earpiece that the team hidden in the national park had sight of four ATVs moving toward their position. They would reach the shed within minutes. The senior officer radioed all team members to standby.

Moments later, some eerie bobbing lights appeared in the distance, breaking through the treeline and travelling along the dry riverbed. Mikey couldn't see them once they passed into the craggy gully, but he was surprised at how silent the vehicles were. The ATVs must have been electric powered, which explained why he hadn't heard any motors running whenever he had seen the mysterious lights at night.

Mikey's heart was beating so hard, it was all he could hear. In the still darkness, all he could see was the long grass in front of his face and the infinite blackness that surrounded him. He was scared and the adrenaline coursing through his veins was making him shake all over.

Suddenly he heard the voice of the senior officer on the radio calling for the tactical team to move in. Through the darkness, Mikey heard shouting and heavy footsteps moving away from him. He lay flat on the ground, face down, and prayed that Wayne would be safe. A cacophony of raised voices filled the air.

"POLICE! DROP THE WEAPONS!" shouted one voice.

"WHAT THE FUCK?" an angry voice replied.

"On the ground! Do it now!" another voice called out.

The shouting voices began to overlap. Mikey couldn't tell who was saying what. All he could do was listen and hope everything turned out alright.

"Hands behind your back! Don't move!"

"Don't do it! Drop it! Drop it, now!"

A single gunshot cracked like lightning, followed by a terrifying silence. Only the sound of Mikey's rapidly beating heart broke the quiet. Suddenly, heavy footsteps approached rapidly and Mikey held his breath, his body going stiff with terror. A hand clamped down on his shoulder and Mikey gasped as he was flipped over. Wayne looked down at him, smiling broadly. Mikey laughed with relief, his whole body still shaking.

"It's over. We've got them." Wayne said triumphantly.

"Oh, thank goodness. You scared the living shit out of me!"

"Sorry, I didn't mean to startle you. Come on, get up. The team has secured the suspects."

"Was someone shot?" Mikey asked, still spooked by the sound of the gunshot.

"Just a warning shot. One of the suspects tried reaching for his gun. Nobody was hurt."

Relief washed over Mikey like a wave. The two men dusted themselves off and walked down toward the riverbed. As they approached the gully, Mikey saw the four ATVs parked in front of the now open shed, along with four masked individuals. They were kneeling with their arms secured behind them with plastic cuff ties. Mikey instantly recognised the third suspect as the tall, bulky gunman he had encountered earlier that day.

The senior officer pulled off the black knitted ski masks the suspects were wearing one by one. Mikey didn't recognise the first two suspects, but when the third suspect's face was unveiled, Mikey knew him instantly. Robbo, the rural fire chief and Wayne's old friend. Mikey looked at Wayne, and it was obvious he was shocked at this development. The final suspect was unmasked and Mikey was stunned to see it was a woman.

Sandra Harrison, the owner of the antique and furniture shop.

Mikey couldn't believe this kind, helpful woman could be involved in something like this, but her face which had once been sweet and gentle was now scowling at Mikey with an expression of fury that was beyond belief.

"You had to get involved, didn't you? You stupid city fuckwit!" Sandra bellowed as she attempted to stand, but was instantly held in place by a police officer standing behind her.

"Get these four out of here." The senior officer ordered and the four suspects were escorted away.

"It seems we were right about the shed." Wayne said a few minutes later after taking a quick look around the interior of the mysterious structure, "There's a full drug lab in there along with all sorts of chemicals and ingredients for producing meth. Plus there's a huge haul of the finished product, wrapped up and ready to transport. There's likely several million dollars worth of drugs in there."

Mikey was gobsmacked. But then suddenly he was very worried about this development.

"This is all on my land. I'm not going to be held responsible for any of this, am I?"

"No," Wayne chuckled, "I think it's safe to say this was all set up long before you moved in. Plus you came straight to me to report everything. You don't have anything to worry about."

Relief flooded his system. Not just because he wasn't going to be charged with having a drug lab on his property, but because the whole police operation had gone down smoothly and without a drop of blood spilled. He was safe, the tactical team was safe and, most importantly, Wayne was safe.

"What happens now?" Mikey asked.

"Now, we let the team secure the scene. The narcotics task force will process everything and take away the contents of the shed. But right now, you and I are free to head off back to the ranch. I don't know about you, but I'm starving." Wayne said, smiling broadly.

"Me too," Mikey giggled, "Let's go home."

Epilogue

WAYNE WAS EXCITED to leave work and share the good news with Mikey. After several weeks of waiting, he'd finally received word back that afternoon from the big bosses in Melbourne. Things were about to change at Cooper's Landing Police, starting with his uniform.

A change had been in the air ever since the drug bust at the Riverside Ranch six months earlier. Wayne still had trouble believing one of his oldest friends, Robbo, had been involved in something like that. But his quick confession and guilty plea left no room for doubt that the Rural Fire Service chief was not the man Wayne thought he was.

Robbo, Sandra Harrison and their two co-accused all made full confessions and were sentenced to lengthy prison terms. Apparently, Robbo had been hiding a serious gambling problem and gotten way over his head with a local bookie. He ended up taking a job with Harrison as an enforcer, and his position as fire chief helped to give the drug ring information about when they could and couldn't transport their merchandise through the national park and via the abandoned highway.

The drug ring had managed to run successfully for several years without issue, mainly due to the decision not to sell or distribute their product in Cooper's Landing itself. The small town was a hive of gossip and rumour, and the suspects knew that once false move would have their clandestine activities broadcast across the community in no time.

It was Mikey's purchase of the Riverside Ranch that ultimately brought the whole scheme undone. No longer free to move unnoticed on the property, the drug ring tried to scare the city boy away, but in the end, failed.

During their lengthy confessions to the narcotics task force, the suspects revealed that the shed on Mikey's property was only one of three in the area, but it was by far the biggest. The other two smaller sheds were mainly used for storage and, like the shed discovered by Mikey, were eventually located, raided, emptied and dismantled.

Now that the case was closed, and life in Cooper's Landing was finally back to normal, Wayne was relieved to go back to the humdrum tasks of highway patrol and sorting out minor neighbourhood disagreements. Once he had craved a little action in his work, but after experiencing it first-hand and seeing it endanger the life of someone he cared deeply about, Wayne was happy to return to the role of a country cop in a peaceful little town.

When his shift was finally over, he headed straight over to the Riverside Ranch and parked his 4WD around the side of the main house. It was dusk, and he knew from experience that his man would be on the back porch, paintbrush in hand, capturing the glorious sunset onto canvas. As he walked around the back of the house and stepped up onto the porch, he was proven correct as he saw Mikey putting the finishing touches on his latest artwork.

Mikey spotted him and smiled. He put down his paintbrush, wiped his hands on a rag and greeted him with a big hug and a swift kiss.

"How was your day, Sergeant?"

"Amazing. Oh, and you can't call me that anymore."

Mikey's eyes went wide. "Oh my God! You mean, you got it?"

"I got it. My promotion came through this afternoon. You're looking at a freshly minted Senior Sergeant." Wayne said with pride.

Mikey cheered, congratulated him and gave Wayne another big hug and kiss.

"Does this mean I have to salute you from now on?" Mikey said with a cheeky grin.

"No, it just means you can never disobey me," Wayne smirked.

"Yeah, good luck with that." The city boy snorted as he went over to his easel and began packing up his equipment for the day.

"That's not the big news. Seems the whole drug bust stuff has put Cooper's Landing on the map with the big wigs in Melbourne. Given it was the biggest narcotics haul in the state's history, they've decided Cooper's Landing Police will be getting a few upgrades."

"Upgrades?" Mikey asked, looking puzzled.

"Oh yeah. Soon I'll be getting two new officers, including a full-time constable to take over the watch house duties. I won't be on call 24/7 anymore!"

"That's fantastic!" Mikey said, smiling wide, "So, when do the new officers arrive?"

"In a few weeks. Although, I may get one of them sooner than that if the transfer request gets approved. Constable Tran has expressed interest in the watch house position. If his boss at Bushman's Pass and the big bosses in Melbourne approve, he could be starting as soon as next weekend."

Once all of his painting supplies were packed up, Mikey and Wayne carried everything inside to the art studio. The room, which had once been empty, was now filled with completed canvases. Each a beautiful landscape image depicting the ranch, local landmarks and, in one exceptional peace, the beauty spot Wayne had taken Mikey to on their first date.

"We should go out and celebrate." Mikey said, "How about a nice meal down at the diner?"

"I was thinking maybe we could have a quiet night in. Well, maybe not too quiet..." Wayne felt himself blush.

"Oh, I see. Well, did you bring your handcuffs? Because I've been a bad boy and you may have to take me 'down town'" Mikey said with a mock sultry voice and gave him an exaggerated wink. He burst out laughing after a few seconds, clearly very amused by his terrible joke. Wayne looked at him sternly and held up his cuffs.

Mikey instantly stopped laughing and gulped, his eyes going wide as they locked onto the metal restraints. Wayne gave him a wicked smile, and both men started laughing again.

"I love you, city boy."

"I love you too. But you'll never take me alive, copper!" Mikey said, a naughty gleam in his eye as he dashed away toward the main bedroom, Wayne hot on his heels.

~

THE FOLLOWING MORNING, Mikey woke up bright and early. He didn't want to disturb Wayne, so he quietly got out of bed and left his lover to sleep in. Mikey headed to the kitchen to make some coffee and start work on putting together breakfast.

The last six months had flown by, with so much happening in such a short time. The trial for the drug runners had been swift since everyone involved had pleaded guilty. It was only at the trial that the full story was finally revealed of what had been happening behind closed doors in Cooper's Landing.

Sandra Harrison had been going broke trying to keep her family's old antique shop from going under. In a final, desperate attempt to save the shop from closure, Sandra had turned to some loan sharks in Bushman's Pass. Before she knew what was happening, she found herself in some pretty serious debt to some very dangerous people.

She was soon being forced by the loan sharks to traffic drugs in order to pay off her debts. Eventually, she decided to go into 'business' herself, producing and distributing meth, with help from a few contacts she had made in Bushman's Pass. Using the antique shop as a front for laundering money, Sandra was soon doing a roaring trade and her debts were quickly paid off.

Her son, Travis, was completely in the dark about his mother's secret life as the local drug lord and had been left devastated when Sandra had been arrested. The antique shop and its contents, along with his mother's house were repossessed by the police as proceeds of crime. Thankfully, Travis had his own house, otherwise, he would have been left homeless.

Nobody in town held Sandra's crimes against Travis. The whole town had been shocked that one of their own could be the kingpin behind such nefarious activities. The community rallied together to offer Travis all the support he needed, now that he was unemployed and without any family in town. It seemed everyone in Cooper's Landing found little odd jobs and temp work for Travis until he could find himself some full-time employment. Mikey had been stunned at how quickly the town had come together to help one of their own. Nothing like that would have happened back in Melbourne. Mikey was, not for the first time, glad he chose to leave the big city behind.

Just as the coffee was ready and the toast popped out of the toaster, a sleepy Wayne emerged from the bedroom. He came behind Mikey as he was buttering the toast, wrapped his arms around him and started kissing Mikey's neck.

"Good Morning," Mikey said, smiling as Wayne found that sweet spot behind his ear.

"Morning," Wayne said, giving him a playful bite, making Mikey gasp.

"Before you get too carried away, I need my coffee."

Wayne grumbled but accepted a steaming cup of coffee while Mikey brought a big plate of toast over to the kitchen table.

As they ate, Mikey heard several trucks and work vehicles drive down the recently resurfaced driveway, headed toward the service road. They were bound for the worksite about halfway between the ranch and the northern boundary. Wayne grimaced at the noise, but Mikey simply smiled to himself, comforted by the familiar sound of traffic.

Mikey had given the issue of the reducing population of Cooper's Landing some serious thought over the last few months and eventually hatched a plan to try and reverse the town's fortunes. His idea was to open an organic egg farm on his property.

Since the land wasn't suitable for traditional farming or ranching, and there was plenty of space on his property, Mikey had decided to invest some of his savings by building a large industrial shed and raising free-range hens. He knew from experience that organic free-range eggs sold for a mint in the city, and he had the money to invest in a quality operation that made use of solar power, sustainable water reclamation technology and organic farming methods. Construction began a few months earlier, and if all went according to plan, the Cooper's Landing Organic Egg Farm was set to open for business in around six months.

While Mikey freely admitted he wasn't a farmer by any means, he was happy just investing in the operation. He had employed a team of experienced locals to oversee the egg farm's construction and management on his behalf, while he focused on his true passion – his art.

An added bonus would be the egg farm would provide employment not only for the contractors building the farm facilities but to a significant number of locals looking for full-time work on the egg farm. In time, the operation would likely encourage people to move to Cooper's Landing, while encouraging locals looking for work to stay in town rather than move to the city. Building the egg farm was Mikey's way of thanking the town that had so kindly welcomed and accepted him.

He knew the egg farm was unlikely to turn a profit anytime soon, but that didn't concern Mikey in the slightest. Money wasn't everything. Sometimes, you just have to do something crazy if you want to change things for the better. After all, following his bliss had gotten him this far, and the journey had brought him richer rewards than money could ever buy.

He put down his coffee mug, leaned in and gave Wayne a long, deep kiss, knowing that his country cop was all the bliss he needed.

THE END

Don't miss out!

Visit the website below and you can sign up to receive emails whenever Alex Leslie publishes a new book. There's no charge and no obligation.

https://books2read.com/r/B-A-CCJI-USQPB

BOOKS 2 READ

Connecting independent readers to independent writers.

About the Author

Alex Leslie is an Australian-born author of Gay M/M romance works including *Chasing The Cupcake Boy, Hearts Unfrozen, Following His Bliss* and *My Big Gay Family Christmas Fiasco.*

Alex lives with his partner, two troublesome cats (who love sleeping on his laptop!) and is currently dealing with an ongoing addiction to iced coffee drinks.

Read more at www.alexleslieauthor.com.